Murder in Red Rock Canyon
The Rhonda Pohs Mysteries Book Five

Sherry Derr-Wille

ISBN: 978-1-62420-791-4

Credits
Cover Artist: Designs by Ms G
Editor: Amanda Armstrong

Dedication

I would like to dedicate this book to my many fans who have been requesting murder mysteries for the past several years.

Chapter One

Rhonda Pohs glanced in the side mirror of her vehicle as they crossed the state line between Wisconsin and Illinois on I-90. She and her husband, Mark, were on their way to Las Vegas where he was going to be starting a new job.

Behind her was the lifetime she'd spent in Wisconsin along with her career as a homicide detective with the Rock County Sheriff's Department. She thought back over the past four years. After graduating from the Police Academy at Blackhawk Technical College, she'd been hired on as the token woman with the Milton Police Department. At the time, she was thrilled to be doing police work. It didn't take long to realize she wouldn't get the chance to do more than run the speed trap on the highway and do death notifications. Thinking back, if it hadn't been for having to make a death notification, she would have never become involved in a high-profile murder investigation.

With her first case solved, she was hired on with the county. Being the newest detective on the force and a woman to boot, her first partner, Phil Mason, was the one saddled with her. Despite his concerns about working with a woman, they soon became fast friends, especially after working two high profile cases with her as the lead detective. Phil was lucky enough to have gotten a position in Madison with better pay, to say nothing of regular hours, leaving her with yet another new partner, Martin Alexander. She was just getting used to him when he went to the hospital for emergency surgery. She finished her career with the county partnering with Bob Masters.

Now all of that was behind her and her future loomed ahead of her. While Mark was going to be working full-time as soon as they arrived, she faced the uncertainty of unemployment.

"A penny for your thoughts," Mark said.

"Just thinking about the past and contemplating the future. What if I don't get a job in law enforcement in Nevada?"

"I'm sure that's not going to be a problem. Of course, didn't you say you would like to try dealing Blackjack at one of the casinos?"

For the first time since pulling out of town this morning, she started to laugh. "Oh, sure, I'm such a big gambler, I never even went when you and your friends would take off on your little trips to Ho Chunk at the Dells. I have a little knowledge of the game, but don't think I'd be good enough to work in one of the casinos. Maybe I could get a job at a convenience store. If anyone tried to rob me, I'd be able to make a citizen's arrest."

Once they cleared Rockford on I-90 they turned onto I-39 and headed toward St. Louis. Rhonda watched the scenery and gasped when a wind farm loomed on their right.

"I need to stretch my legs," Mark said as he pulled off at the Paw Paw rest area. "Why don't you see if they have anything worthwhile in the vending machines?"

Rhonda agreed and, after using the ladies' room, plugged money into the machines getting them soda, chips and candy bars.

"Do you have any idea how fat we're going to get if this is what we live on for the entire trip to Las Vegas?" she teased.

"This is just snacky stuff. It's still early enough I figure we should be in St. Louis by noon. That should put us about halfway to our destination for tonight. Maybe we can even see the arch before we move on. That should give us enough rest time."

Rhonda smiled at how Mark so carefully planned this trip. He told her he didn't want to drive more than five hundred miles in one day. The first leg would be four hundred and ten miles, giving them time for sightseeing in St. Louis before turning onto I-70 for the drive to Hallsville, Missouri. Mark had everything planned out but other than giving her the names of the towns where they were stopping, he gave her no idea of where they would be staying.

Upon leaving Hallsville, they were planning the longest leg of the trip, to another small town she'd never heard of, Dighton, Kansas. Along the way they would be going through Kansas City. She rather liked the idea of Mark finding small towns for them to spend the nights.

From there they would head for Glenwood Springs, Colorado. With luck she could talk him into stopping in Denver so she could do a little shopping.

The last leg of their trip would take them to Las Vegas. Since they would be getting in late, Mark made reservations for them at the Tropicana for the weekend. A friend who was a high roller promised to make free rooms available for them so they could rest before they got to work on moving into their new home.

"Do we have to stay in the hotel on the strip?" Rhonda asked.

"It's a gift from Tyson, honey. He wants to show us a good time. I've known him since we were kids. He's one of those guys who can fall into a bucket of shit and come out smelling like roses. This is one guy we can benefit by knowing."

"Just how is it you know him?"

"His mom went to high school with my mom. They were and still are best friends. As for Tyson, he's a high-powered salesman working for a company that makes video poker machines for the Indian casinos. He wants to show us a good time before we need to get to work."

Rhonda thought about her mother-in-law's friend, Ellen, Tyson's mother. They'd met a couple of times when Ellen returned to Wisconsin from California. The woman and her husband loved to travel and told how they had been on all seven continents.

Rather than dwelling on what would happen once they got to Nevada, Rhonda concentrated on the small town in Missouri where they would be spending the night.

"Aren't you going to tell me where we're going to be staying?" Rhonda asked.

"That would spoil the surprise. I told you before we left Wisconsin this was going to be a week of pampering for you. I checked out all the places we would be staying when I drove out to leave the truck at the new house a couple of weeks ago. I've had fun planning this surprise for you, so don't try to spoil it for me."

"Whatever you say, but I'm still curious."

It was past noon when they arrived in St. Louis. After a leisurely lunch, they waited in line for the ride to the top of the Arch. Rhonda was awed by the view from the top of the symbol of St. Louis. In a way she wished they would be spending more time in the area, but they had their reservations for tonight all set and their sightseeing would need to be abbreviated.

It was almost dark when they pulled off the highway and into the driveway for the Victorian Country Inn. The beautiful home shouted elegance. Their hostess, Miss B, led them to the Garden Spa Suite and Rhonda felt as though she was in heaven. The king-sized bed looked comfortable and the room's spa seemed to be calling her name.

After driving all day, they were both ready for a relaxing evening. "We'll be staying here for two nights," Mark announced. "Since we're not on a tight schedule I want to check out the area and this place seemed like it's ideal. They put on murder mystery plays and one of the rooms even has a secret passageway. Unfortunately, it was already booked, so I thought this might be one you'd enjoy even more."

Rhonda wrinkled her nose. "I'm just as glad the secret passage room was booked. For some reason, I'm not all that excited about murder mysteries on the trip." She winked broadly at Mark. "The way I'm feeling right now, maybe it's a good thing I don't have a job to go to. It could be a good thing if I have some time away from police work to wind down."

"Sure thing. I know you, honey. When it comes to law enforcement, you're like the proverbial old fire horse. You get one whiff of a murder and you're off and running ready to solve it. That said, I'm glad there's no murder mystery scheduled while we're here. None of the other guests would have a snowball's chance to solve it."

Rhonda agreed but pretended to pout. It didn't take long for Mark to take her in his arms and lead her to the spa so the two of them could relax.

~ * ~

After two nights in the luxurious accommodations at the Victorian Country Inn, Rhonda reluctantly bid their hostess goodbye as they left for their next destination, Dighton, Kansas.

For some reason, Mark wasn't interested in any sightseeing along the way. "Why not stop and see some of the scenery?" she finally asked.

"Because, my nosey little wife, the place the two of us will be staying at for the next couple of nights will have enough sightseeing to satisfy you. I'm so excited about our next stop I can hardly keep from telling you."

Rather than pressure her husband, Rhonda studied the map they'd picked up at the first visitors' center they'd come to when they entered the state. Finding Dighton proved to be a challenge, but she finally located it at the junction of Highways 4 and 23. To say this was an out of the way place was an understatement.

When they finally reached their destination, Rhonda was thrilled to see the quaint farmhouse where they would be spending the next two nights.

Opal Roberts greeted them and escorted them to their room. It wasn't the luxurious theme room from the first bed and breakfast they'd stopped at, but it held a rustic beauty that intrigued Rhonda.

When Opal told them of all the things the Wildhorse Canyon Inn was close to, Rhonda was thrilled. Thoughts of being a child and playing cowboys and Indians with her friends filled her mind.

It didn't take long for Rhonda to change to hiking clothes and shoes so they could walk to the canyon where the bed and breakfast took its name. She could envision the plains Indians of the area chasing the wild horse herds into the canyon where they could capture new stock to add to their corrals. As the sun sank slowly to the west, she drank in the beauty of the area.

"I wish we could take this scenery with us. This is one of the most beautiful places I've ever been."

Mark laughed and snapped a picture of Rhonda silhouetted against the beauty of the canyon bathed in the light of the setting sun.

"See," he said, showing her the image he'd just caught on disk, "now you can have this scenery forever. I think this is one of the best photos I've ever taken of you. Just think of the pictures we can get tomorrow when we go to Dodge City. I can be Matt Dillon to your Miss Kitty."

"I think you have it a little backward. I'm the cop, although I don't think there were many female marshals in the Old West."

They both shared a laugh before heading back to the ranch. Opal suggested they drive into town to get something to eat before returning for the night.

The next morning, after a big breakfast, they left to explore Dodge City, Fort Hayes, Castle Rock and the beautiful chalk spire Pyramids. Every western Rhonda ever read or watched came to life for Rhonda as the day progressed.

~ * ~

Even though Rhonda knew all her fantasies had to come to an end, she didn't want to say goodbye to the beauty of the area. She knew she would miss the hospitality of Marvin and Opal Roberts. She knew the future lay ahead of them and yet another bed and breakfast beckoned them.

"Where will we be spending the night tonight?"

Rhonda knew Mark wasn't about to tell her the name of the place they would be staying, but hoped he would at least give her a city name so she could trace their trip on the map.

Mark had a mischievous smile on his face. "Ah, let's see. I can't tell you the name of the place but it is near Glenwood Springs, Colorado and it's on the National Registry of Historic Places."

Rhonda let her imagination run away with her as they drove through the beauty of the Kansas and Colorado countryside. The words National Registry of Historic Places echoed in her mind bringing with it images of more of the westerns she enjoyed as a child.

At long last they approached the Four Mile Creek Bed and Breakfast and a rustic old red barn greeted them.

"When I stopped here on the way out a couple of weeks ago, I picked up some great literature. This barn was built in 1919. I could have reserved a suite in the barn or one of the cabins, but I opted for a room in the main house with a private bath. We don't need that much room and I thought you'd enjoy being in the main house in a cozy private room just for us."

Rhonda got out of the vehicle and went around to where Mark stood. "It's perfect," she said, as she put her arms around his neck and gave him a kiss.

"Welcome to Four Mile Creek," a man said.

Rhonda turned to see their host coming toward them.

"I'm Jim Hawkins. It's good to see you again, Mark. I've got your room ready. You must be Rhonda. Mark told me how he'd been planning this trip for you on his way out to Nevada. I have to admit, I was intrigued about having a homicide detective staying here and did some digging on the internet to see what I could find out about you."

Rhonda blushed. "Not much to tell, just doing my job. I'm excited to see everything this place has to offer."

"Not a lot of things to do here, but relaxation is something that should be on the top of your list. Considering our weather is still rather warm, I think you'll enjoy hiking in the area and strolling the grounds. Of course, we can offer you some great shopping in the Bunkhouse Mercantile. From what Mark told me a couple of weeks ago, once you get to Las Vegas you won't have much time to relax."

Thoughts of getting to Las Vegas in two days and facing an uncertain future crowded Rhonda's mind. *Yes, I'll most certainly take time to relax here. It's been a long time since I've had to scrounge for a job.*

Chapter Two

Two days later they crossed into Nevada at Mesquite on I15. Signs now started advertising hotels and attractions in and around Las Vegas, including a state park Rhonda never heard of before, Valley of Fire.

"I know it's a bit of a drive," Rhonda said, once she saw the sign, "but that's one place I'd like to visit."

"I figured as much, so I picked up some information on the area. You're definitely in Indian country now. From what I've read, there was a Paiute Indian named Mouse who roamed the area that's now the park. The settlers in the area called him an outlaw, but he caused no trouble with his own people. I'm hoping we can go there in the spring when the cactus is in bloom. The weather should be perfect for hiking. I hear they even have petroglyphs."

Rhonda considered the remnants of a primitive people she would soon be able to see. In the past she'd been enthralled with the documentaries she saw on the History Channel. Now she would be able to study them firsthand and experience the magic she equated with the messages from the ancients.

"We're pulling into North Las Vegas," Mark announced, breaking into Rhonda's thoughts about the sightseeing they would be doing in the near future.

With evening falling around them, the lights of the famous city in the desert seemed like a magnet to Rhonda. They'd been there for a couple of days after she wrapped up her last case, but then they'd only spent one day at a small hotel close to the house they were buying. They'd driven down the strip and she'd been entranced by the excitement generated by the city that never seemed to sleep.

"We're right on time," Mark said.

"I didn't know we had a time schedule."

"We don't, but Tyson said his plane would be in from Spokane around six and he's planning to meet us at eight at the Tropicana. It will give us time to get parked and into the hotel. He's going to get us checked in and set us up with money for us to gamble."

Rhonda wasn't as excited about the gambling as Mark but was looking forward to spending time with Tyson. He'd hinted about having ties to Las Vegas' famed Metro police force. Even though she wanted to find work on her own merits, she knew a little help from her friends wouldn't hurt.

Inside the Tropicana, music combined with the clanging of slot machines to set the stage for the magic of Vegas. The one thing to make Rhonda uncomfortable was the idea of people being able to smoke, not only cigarettes but also cigars in the casino.

"Guess I'm too used to the laws in Wisconsin that say you can't smoke in bars and restaurants," she commented, as she wrinkled her nose.

"I'm sure we'll get used to it. To misquote Dorothy from the Wizard of Oz, 'we aren't in Wisconsin anymore'."

Rhonda was about to say something more when Tyson joined them. "I see the two of you made it. Did you have a good trip?"

"The last leg was a long one," Mark said as they shook hands.

Even though Rhonda met Tyson a couple of times, it surprised her when he gave her a brotherly hug as well as a kiss on the cheek.

"Let's get you checked into the hotel and settled in your room. Once we get that done, we're going out to dinner."

Rhonda and Mark followed Tyson into the players' lounge where a lovely young lady with dark hair, bright red lipstick, a form fitting black dress and five-inch heels met them. She motioned them to the snacks set up on a sideboard and invited them to help themselves not only to the snacks but also to the bottled water available to them.

Once Tyson finished the paperwork, he handed Rhonda a key to go up to their room while he and Mark went out to get the luggage they brought with them. Stepping into the elegant elevator, Rhonda thought about what Mark said about not being in Wisconsin anymore. She was in an elegant hotel and heading for the fourteenth floor and the room reserved in their name for the next three nights.

From the window of the room, the lights of the strip looked more like a decorated Christmas tree than sin city. To her left, she saw the shaft of light coming from the top of the pyramid shaped Luxor hotel. Just seeing the beam going straight up in the air made her wonder if the track of light would signal a UFO to descend from the heavens.

"Are the accommodations to your liking?" Tyson asked as soon as the door to the room opened.

Rhonda turned, nodding her approval. "This is beyond what I expected. Are you sure…?"

"Positive. Now, I hope you're hungry. Mark and I were talking on the way up and we're starved."

Rhonda glanced at the clock on the dresser and realized it was almost ten at night. Even though they'd stopped for a late lunch it had been seven hours since they last ate. "Sounds good to me."

Without putting anything away, the three of them went down to the restaurant on the far side of the casino. Once they placed their order, Tyson told them to make certain they took advantage of the breakfast buffet the next morning and to charge their meals to the room.

"I know this is your vacation time," Tyson said as they enjoyed their entrees.

Rhonda immediately stopped eating and focused her attention on Tyson. Was he going to tell her about the possibility of a job?

"I was talking to my friend at Metro, and she told me there's a moratorium on hiring for the department. I'm sorry. I'd hoped to be able to get you an interview with them. I'm still looking into possibilities for you with Clark County and the State Patrol."

Rhonda didn't know if she should be relieved or disappointed. She wanted to get into police work, but she wasn't certain she wanted to be in a city the size of Las Vegas. Her experience in Wisconsin had been focused in a more rural setting. Even when she worked on the Milton Police Force, it was little more than a wide spot in the road compared to this.

"What kind of connections do you have with the local convenience stores? Maybe I'm not cut out for detective work in the big city."

Her question brought laughter from both Mark and Tyson, but in reality, she was completely serious.

"Yeah," Mark responded, "like that's going to happen. I told you, you're like an old fire horse. It won't take long until you're ready to get back to what you love. For now, enjoy the reprieve and relax."

"Well, that's enough about serious things. Between Mark and me we've been talking about what I've got planned for you for your stay. Tomorrow we're going out to see Hoover Dam. We'll be back to the hotel in time for the two of you to get dressed to go out to a show."

"What are we going to see?" Mark looked at Rhonda and winked broadly.

"Have you heard about the show Divas?"

"Who hasn't?" Rhonda inquired. "My former partner was out here this past summer and it was one of the shows he went to with his wife. I've heard the female impersonators are some of the best in the country."

"Good. I didn't think you'd be interested in it. I'm glad you like my choice of shows. Now is there anything else you'd like to do before you get down to everyday life?"

Rhonda thought for a moment. "I'd like to do the zip line down on Fremont Street. I hear it's great."

Both guys looked at her as though they were shocked by her request.

"What's wrong? Isn't it something I should be doing?"

Tyson laughed. "I haven't done it myself, but my mother says it's a real blast. Why don't you and Mark do that the day after the show, then come to my loft for brunch and a dip in the pool? It would make for a good way to spend your last day of vacation since the next morning, Mark tells me you'll be going out to your house so he can start work on Monday."

With dinner finished, Mark and Tyson opted to enjoy the casino. "Don't you want to join us, honey?"

Rhonda stifled a yawn. "I think I'll head up to bed. You know how I get when we travel, it really wears me out. Besides, I'm sure the two of you will have more fun without me. I'm not much of a gambler. Have fun and just remember don't keep me waiting for breakfast in the morning."

Mark gave her a kiss and promised not to wake her when he returned to the room.

~ * ~

Rhonda felt as though she'd been on a non-stop rollercoaster ride. By the time she and Mark waited in line for the zip line, she felt as though she'd been treated more like a queen than a common tourist.

"Are you sure this is what you want to do?" Mark's face looked a little white.

"Of course it is. Phil and Judy said it was a real rush. Don't tell me you're scared?"

"Okay, I won't, but you know how I feel about heights."

"What are you going to do tonight when we go to the top of the Stratosphere?"

"Tyson tells me they have happy hour two for one martinis and we'll be there in time to enjoy them. I plan to get happily sloshed before we go up to the very top. I hope you're not planning to jump off the top."

"Believe me, I'm not that adventurous. I'm just curious about what it's like. I know we're going to be living out here and can go any time, but this is a lot more fun. Besides, when will we ever have such a knowledgeable tour guide like Tyson to show us the ropes?"

The line moved forward, and the attendant motioned for Mark and Rhonda to come and get into the harness. Her heart beat in anticipation as they stepped onto the platform from where they would ride down the line over the busy street below.

"Sit back like you're on a swing," the young man, who hooked them up to the line for the ride of a lifetime, told them.

When she picked up her feet and leaned into the harness that was now attached to the line she wondered about her sanity for the first time. Before she had time to have more than one second thought, she found herself zipping along the metal cable line toward the platform on the other end of the street. Never before had she felt such exhilaration.

Once their feet touched the solid platform, Rhonda looked at Mark and saw the excitement in his eyes. "You had a great idea, honey. It's too bad we're on a tight schedule, I'd like to go again. They said it was only a little bit extra."

Rhonda hugged him tightly. "It's not like we won't ever be able to come back. I have to admit that was a thrill. For now, we're expected at Tyson's place for brunch. After this little adventure I'm starving. Besides, he told me has a wonderful collection of wine. I'm anxious to see what he's planning to serve us with brunch."

After purchasing pictures to prove they'd ridden the zip line, they made their way to Tyson's loft. The building was impressive, but Rhonda was glad she didn't want to live in a high-rise building, even with a pool and hot tub on the roof. It was a great experience, but she was looking forward to moving into their new home.

Brunch was a buffet of fixings for tacos as well as taco salad. To go with it was almond champagne. After relaxing in the pool and hot tub, Rhonda enjoyed sitting on the balcony, basking in the warmth of the late afternoon sunshine. She hardly realized she'd dozed off until Mark came out and said it was time to go to the Stratosphere for drinks and dinner.

Chapter Three

Rhonda's dream vacation on the Vegas strip was nothing more than a beautiful memory. Mark started his job three weeks earlier and the task of settling into their new home fell to her.

When they were in Las Vegas earlier, they'd purchased furniture which had been delivered the afternoon they moved from the Tropicana to their new home. Over the past few weeks, she'd poked through several shops in the area looking for linens, china, glass ware and knick-knacks to make the home their own.

"What are you planning to do today?" Mark asked over breakfast.

Unbidden tears started to fall. "I'm going to do the same thing I've been doing for the past three weeks. I'll do the dishes, clean a house that doesn't need cleaning and go shopping for things I don't need. Oh, Mark, what if I don't find a job? Will we be able to keep this house?"

"Of course, we will. Give it time. It hasn't been that long. Something will come along. If it makes you happy, why don't you go down to the convenience store and fill out an application?"

Rhonda's tears turned to nervous laughter. "Now you're teasing me. Just get out of here and go to work. I'll find something to do for the rest of the day and have a good supper ready for you when you get home. Maybe I'll go shopping and get the fixings for Black and Blue salad so we can use up the steak that's left over from last night."

~ * ~

After Mark left, Rhonda looked around her gourmet kitchen. She knew it had been a big selling point for Mark. He loved to cook, where she was content to allow him to make their meals. With him working and her at home all the time, she knew she should be cooking for him, but as adventurous as she got was to fix a steak or roast chicken. Come the weekend he would be in second heaven.

She knew, in time, they would cultivate a circle of friends and Mark could show off his culinary talents, but for now she was scrounging to be able to make the simplest of meals.

The last dish was loaded in the dishwasher and the counters wiped down when Rhonda's cell phone rang. Since no one in Las Vegas had the number, she decided it must be someone from back home.

"Pohs here," she automatically answered, knowing whoever was calling her would get a kick out of her sounding like the professional she used to be.

"I'm calling for Rhonda Pohs," the stranger on the other end of the line said.

The shock of not knowing the caller took hold of her mind. She took a deep breath. "This is she."

"I'm Hanna Watson, calling from the HR department for the Clark County Sheriff's Office. When will you be in Las Vegas and available to come in for an interview?"

Immediately it clicked that she'd used the cell phone number on her resumes that were sent out to the local police departments before leaving for Nevada. "I've been in Nevada for the past three weeks. I'm available at any time."

"Could you come in this afternoon, at say two, for an interview?"

"I'll be there, do I ask for you?"

"Yes. I'll be there. I'm looking forward to meeting you."

She hung up the phone and wished she had someone in the area she could call with the news of getting an interview. The only two people she was close to in Vegas were Mark and Tyson and both of them were at work. Still wanting to tell someone, she went to the bathroom to take a quick shower before leaving for her appointment.

~ * ~

"I'm Rhonda Pohs, I have an appointment with Hanna Watson," Rhonda told the officer sitting behind the reception desk.

The young man looked at her and nodded, then picked up the phone to announce her to the woman in the HR department.

I wonder if he thinks I'm here for a job in the secretarial pool.

The woman who came out to the desk to meet her looked to be in her early thirties. Her blonde hair sported a stylish cut, and her suit was of the latest fashion. It made Rhonda wonder if her small town suit from her detective days made her look like a hick from the sticks.

"Captain Brannigan is waiting for you in my office, Ms. Pohs. Won't you follow me?"

The shocked expression on the face of the officer at the desk didn't come as a surprise to Rhonda. "Thank you, Ms. Watson."

They went down a short hall before entering a corner office with windows looking out onto the Nevada landscape.

"Ms. Pohs, it's a pleasure to finally get to meet you," the man sitting in one of the leather chairs in front of the desk said as he got to his feet. "I'm Karl Brannigan."

"It's good to meet you as well. Since you called me, you must have received my resume."

Brannigan picked up a pile of papers from the edge of the desk. "Oh yes, we've received your resume, as well as letters from the chief of police from Milton, WI, the Rock County Sheriff, your former partners and one Tyson Wrensch. If I'm to believe all of these gentlemen, you're someone we'd like working for Clark County. You are still interested in law enforcement, aren't you?"

Rhonda immediately relaxed. "I'm very interested. I must assume you've researched my background."

"I didn't have to. These letters of recommendation all speak very highly of you. I'm thankful there's a hiring freeze at Metro. I doubt I need to tell you Clark County is much bigger than where you've worked before. There's a lot of area to cover. I need someone who can start immediately. One of my homicide detectives took a bullet and I have a position that needs to be filled."

Rhonda's heart skipped a beat. "How would one of your detectives feel about working with a woman?"

Brannigan smiled broadly. "Jennifer Sims is new to the squad, but she's good. With your experience, you'd be primary on any case the two of you work, but I think the two of you will work very well together. If you don't mind filling out the paperwork today, we'd like you to start as soon as possible."

Two hours later Rhonda left the office. Her picture had been taken for an ID badge, the necessary paperwork filled out, and an appointment scheduled for the next day for the mandatory physical required before starting work.

She pulled into the driveway right after Mark parked his truck. Before she could get out of her vehicle, Mark was out to greet her. "Hi beautiful. You look like the cat that swallowed the canary. The way you're dressed, something great must have happened."

"My dear husband, you are now looking at the newest detective for the Clark County Sheriff's Department."

"That was fast. What happened?"

Rhonda related the details of her afternoon interview and subsequent hiring. "I have to have a physical tomorrow and will be starting next Monday."

"That's wonderful, honey. I have a feeling you haven't started fixing supper yet. Let's go out and celebrate. I'll call Firefly and make reservations. It's still early, we can have a nice celebration and still be home before it gets too late. Even if you aren't starting until Monday, I do have to go to work tomorrow."

Together they went into the house and prepared to go out to dinner. On the way back into the city, Rhonda called her old partner Phil Mason to tell him her good news. Calls to the other people who sent letters of recommendation could wait until tomorrow.

Chapter Four

"Happy anniversary," Mark greeted Rhonda when she got up on Sunday morning.

She'd almost forgotten today was their wedding anniversary. She should have planned something, but with all the preparations to start work on Monday morning, the event completely slipped her mind.

"How long have you been up?"

She glanced at the clock and noticed it was after nine.

"Long enough to have the car packed for the surprise I have in store for you."

"Surprise? What kind of surprise?"

"You'll see. It's a good day for hiking, so dress accordingly. When you're ready, we'll be off for a celebration like you never expected."

"So, where are we going?"

"Nope. I'm not telling. You get cleaned up and dressed and we'll have breakfast. Don't dawdle because I'm anxious to be off for the day."

Rhonda knew better than to try to get Mark to tell her a secret. She took a quick shower and dressed in hiking clothes before going down to the kitchen.

Mark had the table set and was just putting French toast on her plate when she sat in the chair he held for her. She hadn't noticed before, but Mark was dressed in shorts, tee-shirt and hiking boots. She was glad she'd picked a similar outfit.

With breakfast finished and the kitchen cleaned up, Mark led her out to his truck. As much as she wanted to look in the box, he had the cover over it, so whatever his plans were had been hidden from her sight.

They headed toward the strip but instead of going into the city, Mark drove back out in the country. Finally, he pulled into the driveway for Red Rock Canyon National Park.

"Oh, Mark, this is perfect. I've been seeing the signs for this place. I even read an article about it in the paper last week."

"I saw that article as well. I knew you'd enjoy this. After talking to some of the other teachers at work, I decided it was a worthwhile field trip for the two of us."

He pulled into the parking lot for the information center. Rhonda entered the building and enjoyed the amount of indoor and outdoor displays. "It all makes me anxious to see the actual canyon for myself."

"So, you shall, my beautiful wife. I hope you're up to doing lots of hiking. We'll have several stops before we get to the picnic area. From what I'm told we can hike in any one of them, but Calico I is a good place to start. We don't have to hike all of them today. It's not like we won't ever be able to come back here again. I thought we'd get some good pictures at most of them."

Rhonda studied the hiking map they'd picked up when they first entered the visitor center. "Oh I want to hike them all, but that would take more time than one day. I do want to see the petroglyphs. They were really emphasized in the article I read in the paper. Can you imagine painting on the rocks, made by an ancient civilization, and still surviving today?"

"They intrigue me, too. From this map I'd say they're about halfway around the circle. If we're going to have time to do some hiking, have our lunch and get time to study the petroglyphs, we'd best get started. Something tells me this won't be the last time we come here. I guess it's a good thing I bought the annual pass when I was out here dropping off the truck."

The drive to Calico I was short, but as soon as they were on the road, Rhonda was entranced by the scenery surrounding them.

Mark no more than pulled into the parking stall than Rhonda unbuckled her seat belt and opened the car door. From the parking area she gasped at the enormity of the cliffs of red rising before them. As much as she wanted to hike the trail, she doubted she was up to climbing the cliffs like the number of people she could see dotting the trail leading up to the top of the rocks.

"Oh, Mark, this is magnificent. I don't know if we'll be able to make it up to the top, though."

"I've never been into the rock-climbing thing. I don't mind the hiking, but I draw the line at risking my life."

Rhonda laughed at his statement, but deep in her heart, she knew more about people risking their lives just by living than he did. She wondered how many intrepid hikers fell to their deaths from the top of the cliffs.

The trail leading to the base of the rocks went downhill at a gentle slope which was paved for the ease of even the least experienced hiker.

"I feel really insignificant down here," she commented as she stood before the beautiful red rocks that leant their name to the canyon.

"I know what you mean," Mark replied. "I think we should ease into the longer hikes."

Rhonda looked up at him and smiled. "I don't think I'm adventurous enough to try climbing up there." She pointed at the kids scrambling up the rocks like miniature mountain goats.

"Good. Let's go back up to the top and move on to the next area."

At one stop after another they parked and got out to take pictures and hike at least some of the trails.

It was just past noon when they arrived at the picnic area. "Picnic first," Mark declared, "then we'll tackle the trail to the petroglyphs."

"It sounds good to me," Rhonda agreed. "I hope you've got something good packed for our lunch. All that hiking has made me hungry."

Mark winked slyly as he started taking not only a picnic basket but also a cooler from the bed of the truck.

From the picnic basket, he pulled plastic plates, silverware and cups along with a bowl of fresh strawberries, as well as one containing finger sandwiches.

"This looks wonderful. Did you bring some bottled water in the cooler?"

"That and more." He opened the cooler and produced a bottle of the same almond champagne they'd enjoyed when having brunch at Tyson's loft. "You liked this so much I asked Tyson where I could get some for our anniversary."

After popping the cork, Mark placed a strawberry in each of the two glasses and poured the wine over the fruit. "There's nothing more romantic than having champagne and strawberries with my beautiful wife. Happy anniversary, Rhonda."

The soft clink of the plastic glasses completed their toast and the sweet taste of the champagne attested to their love for one another. Once they finished their wine and strawberries, Mark kissed her passionately. She marveled at the taste of her husband mingled with that of the wine and fruit.

Mark poured them each another glass and Rhonda reached for one of the finger sandwiches in the plastic container, as a scream rent the air. The police officer in Rhonda forgot about the romance as she was immediately on her feet.

"Someone has fallen," a woman shouted as she ran into the picnic area. "I-I think she might be hurt. She wasn't moving."

Rhonda was immediately at the woman's side. "Where did you see this woman?"

Her shrieks of terror turned to hysterics, trying Rhonda's patience.

"W-We were hiking up to the petroglyphs and my husband saw her just off the trail. I left him there a-and came down here for help."

A small crowd of tourists had begun to gather but no one seemed to be willing to take a leadership position. Rhonda instinctively started barking orders. "I'll go up and see what's going on. While I do, I want someone to see if they can find a park ranger. If anyone can get a signal down here, call 911."

Rhonda headed up the rocky trail, followed closely by Mark. Normally she would have preferred to go alone, but if someone was badly hurt, Mark's expertise would be invaluable. For several years he'd worked on the volunteer fire department and was well versed in first aid.

Unlike the trails they'd walked earlier, this one was strewn with rocks making haste next to impossible. If someone was badly injured, getting emergency personnel up this trail could become a nightmare.

"You're not EMT's," the man whose wife came to alert them to the accident accused. "I told Agnes to call the paramedics."

"Someone is calling 911, sir," Rhonda said. "I'm a police officer. Can you tell me what happened?"

She cringed at the half-truth she'd told. Officially she was a civilian, but in less than twenty-four hours she'd be working for the Clark County Sheriff's Department.

"My wife and I came up to see the petroglyphs and we saw her." The man pointed to the woman lying just off the trail.

Rhonda watched as Mark assessed the condition of the woman, checking for a pulse. To her dismay, he shook his head. Carefully, she picked her way down the slight embankment to where Mark knelt next to the body.

"I doubt she fell," Mark said as he nodded at the blood staining her shirt. "It looks like a stab wound to the heart."

"How can you be so sure? There's not a lot of blood."

"That's because whoever stabbed her knew what they were doing. She was dead instantly and as soon as her heart quit beating, there was no more blood."

"What's going on up here?"

Rhonda turned at the sound of a man's voice. Behind her stood a park ranger she assumed worked out of the aid station she'd seen at one of the stops they'd made earlier in the day.

"I'm Rhonda Pohs. I work for the Clark County Sheriff's Department. Please keep everyone back until the officers can get here. We have a murder."

"Murder?" The man who'd sent his wife for help echoed. "I don't want to be involved in a murder."

Rhonda tried to throttle her exasperation. For the second time in the last hour, she'd stretched the truth.

"I'd suggest you radio back to the station and ask for a homicide detective to come out here. As a matter of fact, I'd like to see if Karl Brannigan and Jennifer Sims could be sent."

Chapter Five

Without crime scene tape to close off the area, Rhonda insisted everyone should go back down to the parking lot. The Park Rangers could keep the curious from going up the rocky trail, while Rhonda talked to Agnes and Kenny Johnson.

"We didn't have anything to do with that mess," Kenny kept insisting.

"I know you didn't, but I'd like to get your information since you were the ones who first discovered the body."

"Do you have to call her 'the body'?" Agnes questioned.

Rhonda took a cleansing breath and tried to explain. "I call her 'the body' because at this minute that's what she is. We don't even know who she is."

Before she could continue, sirens screamed into the area. Two squad cars along with an unmarked vehicle pulled into the parking area along with a fire truck and ambulance.

"Just what in the hell…?" Karl Brannigan stopped in front of Rhonda. "Ms. Pohs, I guess I should have known when dispatch called Jenny as well as me in on this one."

"I probably overstepped my bounds," Rhonda said when she was sure no one else was listening in. "My husband and I were out here celebrating our wedding anniversary when Mrs. Johnson came down to the picnic area. She and her husband were the ones who found the body. Once I realized we had a murder victim, I thought it was best to call you in. Since I was here, I…"

"I get it, you want to be the primary on this one. How did you know it was murder rather than a simple fall?'

"My husband used to work on the volunteer fire department. He was the one who determined the victim was dead. He couldn't get a pulse and…"

"I get the picture detective. Let's get up to the crime scene. Once we get the information we need there we can let the Fire Department take over.

They can take the body back to the coroner's office and we'll see what they have to say. I know you're not officially on the force until tomorrow, but maybe it's time you met your new partner."

He nodded his head toward the young woman dressed in a suit coat and jeans standing next to a second unmarked car.

Together they walked over to where Jennifer stood. "Jennifer Sims, meet your new partner, Rhonda Pohs."

"I hadn't expected us to meet under these circumstances," Rhonda said, extending her hand. "Are you up to hiking up to the crime scene?"

Jennifer smiled. "I was at home when I got the call. As soon as I heard I was supposed to be coming out to Red Rock Canyon, I grabbed my hiking boots. This is one of my favorite spots to hike."

Rhonda knew instantly she and Jenny were going to work well together.

Leaving Mark behind, Rhonda led Jenny and Brannigan back up to the crime scene. The rangers did a good job in keeping the tourists away from the scene and the body remained in the same position where they'd left it.

Knowing a CSI team wouldn't be coming to this remote location, Rhonda started snapping pictures with her cell phone while Jennifer used a digital camera she pulled from her jacket pocket.

"You're way ahead of me on this one," Rhonda commented. "My husband, Mark, and I are so used to snapping pictures on our cell phones, we don't even own a good camera. I'm not used to having to take my own crime scene photos."

"You'll find a lot of things are different here from what you're used to in Wisconsin," Karl said. "Clark County covers a vast area. Sometimes cases take us to places like these that are too remote for the CSI crew to get in easily. It's always best to be armed with your camera just in case of something like this. Your camera will be waiting for you on your desk on Monday morning."

Rhonda nodded, feeling suddenly like the little country mouse who came to the big city. Police work she knew. Having to become her own CSI agent in remote locations was completely alien to her.

"I saw you talking to an older couple when we got here," Karl continued. "Were they the people who found the body?"

"Yes, they are. Their names are Agnes and Kenny Johnson and they're visiting their daughter for the next two weeks. I was able to get the contact information for their daughter and told them we'd be asking them to come into the office to give an official statement."

"I'm impressed," Jenny said. "Do you keep all that information in your head?"

Rhonda instantly relaxed. "Good heaven's no. I always keep a pen and pad in my car. Just reflex, a lot like you carrying your camera. I've worked on four high profile murder cases in Wisconsin as the primary and several more as secondary to my partner. Taking notes comes second nature to me, even when I know the interviews are recorded."

"You mean the taped interviews done in the office," Karl said.

"In the office and in the field. On the last case I worked before relocating, a man was killed on a farm where they were having his twenty-fifth-class reunion. We were lucky the son of the owner of the farm had a recording studio set up in one of the outbuildings."

"Sounds pretty high-tech to me considering you were in the middle of nowhere."

"Rock County is far from the middle of nowhere. It's a farming community, but you're never more than twenty miles from somewhere, be it a small town or a medium-sized city. There's also a lot of manufacturing. I do admit finding a recording studio on a farm was a surprise, since we weren't close to any of the major cities but with the Internet, everything is changing."

"So," Jenny inquired, "is this guy doing anything with his recordings?"

"I wish I could say he is, but before the investigation was finished, he was murdered. It was a complicated case."

The looks on Jenny and Karl's faces mirrored both envy and admiration. "Sounds like you're going to give us a breath of fresh air in the department," Karl said. "I think you and Jenny are going to work well together."

Once back in the parking area, Karl went over to where the other emergency personnel waited for his instructions. After climbing the rock-strewn trail twice in the last hour, Rhonda wondered how the EMT's would be able to retrieve the body.

"Are you okay, honey," Mark said, coming over to put his arm around her waist. "I know you weren't planning to start work until tomorrow, but I understand you have to go when duty calls. We'll have time for more picnics in the future. Just make me proud of you and show these people from Clark County just what they got when they hired you."

Mark's words bolstered Rhonda's ego, but she still regretted the intrusion into their anniversary celebration. Thinking about what Mark planned this day to be, she realized if they hadn't decided to eat before checking out the petroglyphs, they would have been the ones to discover the body at the top of the trail.

Tourists congregated around the emergency vehicles in the parking lot and asked a multitude of questions as the EMT's came back down the trail with the body bag holding the remains of what might have been a wife, mother, sister, or daughter just hours earlier.

Rhonda looked over to where Mark sat, a smile on his face. Behind him she saw the sun sinking behind the red hills. "Do we need to go back to the office?" she asked, silently praying the answer would be no.

"We won't have any information from the coroner's office until morning. Until we know more, she's a Jane Doe. Why don't you and your husband try to salvage what's left of your day."

Rhonda could have hugged Karl. With the lateness of the hour, she doubted if they would do any more hiking today.

Chapter Six

Rhonda thought she would be nervous about starting a new job but having worked with Karl and Jenny on Sunday drove all thoughts of nervous anticipation from her mind.

As promised, a small digital camera, like the one Jenny carried, sat on the desk in her cubicle. She'd just started putting a picture of Mark beside it on the desk, when Jenny arrived.

"Nice picture of your husband," she said in greeting.

"Thanks. I think he's special. Now that we have the pleasantries out of the way, how long do you think we'll have to wait for the report from the coroner's office?"

"It was in my inbox this morning. I printed it off so we could go over it together. By this afternoon IT should have your email set up."

Rhonda motioned to the chair sitting next to her desk and together with Jenny scanned through the printed pages before her. "This confirms Jane Doe was stabbed in the heart, but does this make any sense?"

Rhonda looked at the part of the report Jenny was pointing to. "Why would there be stone chips in the heart?" She took a minute for the impact of the statement to sink in. "Oh my god, she was stabbed with a stone knife. Who uses a primitive tool like that anymore?"

"I certainly haven't heard of any of the Native Americans in the area being on the warpath."

"Maybe not, but the location of the body and the method of the murder sure makes it look that way. Do we have any idea who this woman is?"

"Good question, Detective," Karl said as he entered the cubical. "Missing Persons just contacted me. The way it looks we've had a typical weekend. There's a missing college student from UNLV, a missing tourist from Kansas, and a dealer who didn't show up for work yesterday. From the descriptions, any of them could be our girl. I want the two of you to start checking each of these out."

Rhonda looked at the report Karl handed her. In Wisconsin, there would be maybe one missing person in a month to say nothing of three in a weekend. "Is this normal?"

Karl and Jenny both laughed. "Welcome to Las Vegas, Rhonda," Jenny finally managed to say. "On Monday morning there are usually one or two people who go missing. With the tourists, it's usually because they hooked up with someone or got so drunk they forget where they're staying. So, where do you want us to start, boss?"

"Have you downloaded the pictures from your camera yet?"

Jenny nodded.

"Take a look at them and see if you have a good one of our victim's face. Don't want to be showing these people the more gruesome ones. Once you're done, you can start with the missing tourist. With luck she's back with her hubby and nursing one hell of a hangover."

Rhonda watched as Jenny pulled up her pictures of the crime scene and selected a good facial shot before downloading the pictures from her phone to the hard drive of the department's computer.

"I think this picture you took is much better than mine," Jenny observed. "I'll get several copies of this one printed off before we start interviewing the families. The tourist and her husband are staying at the Luxor so we can start there."

Rhonda read over the missing person's reports while Jenny printed off the pictures they would be showing the families. This was going to be a very different case. Not only was the victim killed with a primitive weapon, she was also an unknown. The other cases she'd worked in the past at least gave her somewhere to start in the investigation. Even with the first case, the identity of the victim was known within hours of discovery of the body. From what she read in the coroner's report, the woman had been dead for at least two hours before she was found by the Johnson's.

The thought of the couple who she'd talked to yesterday prompted Rhonda to open the file on the case and add her handwritten notes before putting the pages from her notebook into the physical file.

~ * ~

Monday morning on the strip seemed much quieter than she'd experienced the first weekend she'd been in town. The raucous partiers often seen in the evening were either sleeping it off or becoming the excited tourists out to see the sights.

From the hotel where they stayed right after arriving, Rhonda remembered seeing the beam of light coming out of the top of the Luxor. Although she'd wanted to visit the pyramid-shaped hotel there just hadn't been time to do everything she and Mark planned before they were ready to move into their new home.

She found the distraught husband in their room near the top of the hotel. "When was the last time you saw your wife?" Rhonda asked.

"We're here with another couple and she went sightseeing with them yesterday. I think they were going to Hoover Dam and Lake Mead. When they weren't back last night, I called to report her missing."

Behind them they heard the click of the door being opened with its electronic key. "Just what is going on?" the woman who entered the room demanded. "I tried to call your cell phone to tell you we were spending the night in Boulder City, but you didn't answer. Did you even check your voicemail before you called in not one but two hookers?"

"Hookers?" the husband shouted. "These women aren't hookers. They're police officers. I reported you as a missing person. I thought you were dead for Christ's sake."

"We're just glad you're alive and well and not the victim we're looking for," Rhonda said, extending her hand to the angry woman. "I hope you enjoy the remainder of your vacation."

Once they were in the hall, Rhonda and Jenny could hear the heated argument between husband and wife going on just behind the closed door.

"Well, that's a first," Jenny said trying hard not to laugh. "I've been called a lot of things but never a hooker. Like how many working girls do you see wearing suits and sensible shoes?"

As soon as Rhonda got into the elevator, she began laughing at the statement. "I agree completely. I've been called a lot of names over the years, but prostitute certainly isn't one of them. Mark's going to get a real laugh out of it."

Once back on the strip, Jenny suggested they go to the Stratosphere to talk to the pit boss about his missing dealer.

"Something tells me, it's going to be another dead end," Jenny commented.

"I know what you mean, but at least they won't mistake us for hookers."

Jenny's prediction came true. Unfortunately, the dealer had been beaten up by her boyfriend and spent the night in the hospital before pressing charges of domestic violence and breaking up with the man.

At the dorm on the UNLV campus, they were met by the parents of the missing girl, the girl's roommate and the detectives from Missing Persons who were interviewing everyone. After introducing themselves, they listened to the questions posed by their Missing Person's counterparts.

"Where do you think our daughter is?"

The mother was crying, but the father was very vocal. It seemed as though he thought by shouting the officers could produce his daughter from thin air.

"That's why we're here," the lead missing persons detective said. "When was the last time you saw Nancy?"

Rhonda was glad she'd familiarized herself with the case, so she knew the missing person was Nancy Callahan.

"That's what I'm asking you," Mr. Callahan said before the roommate could answer.

"I was addressing Nancy's roommate," the detective continued, exasperation sounding in his voice.

"Nancy said she was going to go hiking," Nancy's roommate, Sara, replied. "She asked me if I wanted to go, but I had a date."

Rhonda could feel her heart tighten in her chest. "Where did she like to go to hike?"

"She's a geology major. I think she was going to Red Rock Canyon. She likes to go there to hike and do some rock climbing. She also likes to take pictures."

For a moment, Rhonda thought this was going to be another dead end. There had been no camera found at the scene.

"About noon, she sent me these pictures from her phone."

Rhonda looked at the picture Sara displayed. It showed the petroglyphs at Red Rock Canyon.

"Let me see that," Mr. Callahan demanded.

"Can I send this to my phone, Sara?" Rhonda asked, before handing the phone to Nancy's father.

"Do you have a recent picture of Nancy?" Jenny asked.

Mrs. Callahan nodded and produced a wallet sized picture that must have been taken for Nancy's high school yearbook. The studio posed photo looked stiff and from the date stamped in the lower right-hand corner told Rhonda and Jenny it wasn't current but at least four years old.

"I have some pictures we took last weekend when we went up to Lake Tahoe," Sara said, taking her phone back from Mr. Callahan and flipping through her pictures.

The difference between the two pictures was day and night. In the graduation picture, Nancy wore her hair long and bleached blonde. The one from Sara's phone showed Rhonda as the woman they'd found alongside the trail in front of the petroglyphs in Red Rock Canyon.

"I'm sorry, I'm afraid we have bad news for you. Yesterday we found the body of a young woman. I'm afraid it's Nancy. We do need to have you come down and give us a positive identification."

"No," Mrs. Callahan shouted. "It can't be. Not my daughter. Not my Nancy."

Rhonda ached for Nancy's parents who now found comfort in each other's arms.

"Where do you want us to go, Detective?" Mr. Callahan was finally able to ask, the words hardly louder than a whisper.

"I've made a call, and a squad car will be here in a few minutes to take you to the morgue," Jenny said, taking the burden from Rhonda.

With Jenny making arrangements for Mr. and Mrs. Callahan, Rhonda focused on the pictures from Sara's phone she wanted to have for her use in the case.

"You said Nancy sent you this picture of the petroglyphs," Rhonda commented as she looked closely at the photo of the ancient rock paintings. The image on the phone was small, but soon she would be able to transfer it to her laptop and enlarge it.

"Yes, that's the last I heard from her."

Rhonda looked closer at the photo and realized there was a shadow cast on the rock, as though someone was with Nancy. It was possible this was her killer.

The Missing Persons Squad was just leaving as Rhonda and Jenny excused themselves to go back to headquarters and see what they would find in the pictures now housed on Rhonda's phone.

"Did you find a phone at the crime scene?" Jenny asked once they were in the car.

"I didn't see one. Do you think we'd find it if we went out there?"

"I think you just read my mind. Of course, you aren't dressed for hiking."

Rhonda smiled at the comment. "I took a page out of your book. Yesterday, you said you usually keep a change of clothes for emergencies. I've got shorts and hiking boots in my car at the office. I don't think it will take either of us very long to change so we can go out there and do some poking around."

Chapter Seven

On the way out to Red Rock Canyon, Rhonda and Jenny stopped to have lunch. Back in Wisconsin she would have opted for a burger and fries from a drive through, but here things were different. It didn't take long for her to learn her new partner was a health nut. Jenny insisted on stopping at a sandwich shop and having a turkey wrap with lots of fresh veggies made. Rhonda was pleased to see she could have the same sandwich on bread.

"Don't you like wraps?" Jenny asked once they got bottles of ice-cold water to go along with their lunch and were seated at a table for two.

"My husband would love it if I liked them but to me, they taste like wallpaper paste."

Jenny laughed at the comment. "If you're going to be my partner, you'll at least have to try them. This one is spinach and I think it's exceptional. Since this is your first day I won't push, but you'll find it's much healthier than that bread you're so fond of. That stuff will sit in your stomach like a rock. Being in the desert you'll be learning how to eat light, so you don't get sluggish."

For the first time, Rhonda found the bread to be just as heavy as Jenny said it was. "Okay, but you'll have to give me time to adjust to healthy eating. I'm used to greasy burgers and fries on the fly at lunchtime back home. Guess that's what I get for having male partners who were carnivores."

~ * ~

Being early afternoon on Monday, the park was relatively quiet. The weekend tourists were gone, and the heat of mid-day kept most of the locals away.

After parking the car, Rhonda and Jenny made their way up the rock-strewn pathway leading to the petroglyphs. The yellow crime tape looked like a scar on the ancient landscape.

"Do you think we'll find anything?" Jenny asked once they stood in front to the rock paintings.

"I hope so. I thought it was strange we didn't find any identification on the body. When we first got here, we were warned never to go anywhere without our driver's licenses."

"I thought about that, too. I looked around, but I didn't see anything. It was pretty hectic yesterday. I have to admit, this is my first murder case. I just made detective a month ago."

Rhonda understood. Even though she'd gone into police mode as soon as the body was found, she hadn't thought to look for identification. Back in Wisconsin she would have let the CSI unit look for clues.

"I've got a question for you. Yesterday you said you were into hiking. When you go, where do you carry your phone and ID?"

Jenny thought for a minute. "I usually wear a fanny pack for such things. I know it's not fashionable, but it beats wearing a backpack. I see some of the kids who hike out here but when they go off on the trails, they leave their personal belongings with their folks or in their cars. They don't want to be encumbered by extra weight."

"Cars?" Rhonda repeated the word in the form of a question. "How did Nancy get out here from UNLV? She must have driven. Maybe we could have saved ourselves a long climb. She probably left everything in the car."

"I can buy that, but it still doesn't account for her phone. She sent pictures from the murder site. It has to be here somewhere. As for a car, where is it? I can't believe it would have been left in the park all night without someone taking notice."

Rhonda agreed completely. "I think we need to talk to Sara again and find out what kind of car Nancy was driving. Once we finish here, we'll check with the park rangers and see if there were any cars that were abandoned here last night."

Together they moved off the trail to see if there was anything they missed yesterday afternoon. Rhonda marveled at the stark beauty of the area and at the same time wondered why anyone would choose this barren place to commit such a gruesome murder.

"I think I found something," Jenny called, breaking the pristine stillness of the afternoon.

Rhonda hurried from where she was searching to see what Jenny was talking about. There among the rocks was a cell phone in a camouflage case that almost blended in with its surroundings. From her pocket, Rhonda produced an evidence bag and a pair of gloves before picking up the phone, not contaminating any DNA that might cling to its case.

Once Rhonda held the phone in her hand she stared at the shattered screen. It was apparent when Nancy was attacked, she'd flung it away smashing it against the surrounding rocks. It was entirely possible her attacker wasn't even aware of the phone that could hold incriminating evidence.

Rhonda followed Jenny back down the trail leading to the parking lot. To her amazement no one came up to see the petroglyphs while they'd been there. Even though several vehicles were parked in the lot and people were enjoying the picnic area as well as taking pictures, no one seemed interested in making the climb.

"I'm sure the story about how a body was found here hit the papers this morning," Jenny observed. "It wouldn't surprise me if, not only the locals, but also the tourists are scared to go up there. Maybe it's for the best. If the place had been crawling with tourists, I'm sure we wouldn't have found that phone."

Rhonda nodded her agreement and scanned the parking lot. The one thing to stand out was the yellow VW bug she'd seen the day before parked in the same place. "I have a feeling that VW belongs to Nancy. Do you think we'd be lucky enough that it would be unlocked?"

Jenny shrugged her shoulders and made her way to the car. Rhonda watched as Jenny opened the driver's door. "If Nancy is anything like I was in college, I'm willing to bet I'll find the keys under the floor mat and her driver's license in the glove box."

Rhonda held her breath and prayed this was Nancy's car and they wouldn't be accused of breaking and entering.

"Eureka," Jenny shouted as she held up first the keys then the Nevada driver's license belonging to Nancy Callahan. I'll call back to the office to have a tow truck come out and pick up the car."

Rhonda made certain they locked up the car before going off to find the park ranger on duty. She didn't have to go far before a young man in uniform approached them. She immediately recognized him as the man who had been on duty yesterday afternoon.

"Welcome back to the park," he said, extending his hand. "I'm sure you don't remember me from yesterday. I'm Brent Kramer. I was on duty and helped to keep back the lookers."

"I do remember you, Brent. I'm Detective Rhonda Pohs and this is my partner, Detective Jennifer Sims. Can you tell me why this VW is still in the lot?"

"I just came on duty, but I was told about the car that had been here all night. I wanted to come down and investigate things before I called your office. I guess you were on top of us on this one. Normally, we would have had the vehicle towed this morning, but my morning shift didn't think they should touch it considering what went on here yesterday. They waited until I got in as I'm the senior ranger on duty today."

"I understand completely. Do you have any idea why people aren't going up to the petroglyphs? We were up there this afternoon, and no one even bothered us."

Brent laughed. "I guess the fact someone was murdered up there yesterday hit the media and people are scared off. I don't blame them. I wouldn't want to meet up with some crazed killer. Do you have any line on who it could be?"

Rhonda glanced at Jenny before answering Brent's question. "Nothing we can disclose at this time. We have called for someone to come out and tow the car back to impound."

It was evident Brent was digging for information about what transpired here just twenty-four hours earlier. She knew her reluctance to disclose anything more was disappointing, but she knew from experience the less people who knew the intimate details of a case, the better.

"I have a question for you," Rhonda probed. "Is there another way to get away from the petroglyphs without being seen by the tourists?"

Brent thought for a moment. "There is a way out, but not many people use it. There's a trail that leads to Rocky Gap Road. Like I say it isn't used much because it's the long way around and strewn with rocks. No one can drive in. The only way to get in or out of the back door to the petroglyphs is on foot. I haven't ever tried it, but whoever does has to be an expert."

By the time the tow truck arrived, Brent returned to his duties leaving Rhonda and Jenny alone in the parking lot.

"I know the area he's talking about. I think we need to take a drive over to Rocky Gap Road and see if we can find anything."

Rhonda looked at Jenny. "What do you think we'll find?"

"It's not a well-used road so we might be able to find something we can use. That's the beauty of living in Nevada, we don't have to worry about rain washing away the evidence."

Jenny pulled out of the park and headed toward Rocky Gap Road.

"I think I know where the trail that leads to the petroglyphs is. When I was a kid my friends and I thought we were invincible and hiked all over this area."

She slowed the car down at a pull off area but didn't turn into the small parking area at the head of the trail. "This is it," she declared as she got out of the car. "It's also a great make out spot. I was out here more than once with guys from high school."

Rhonda raised an eyebrow.

"Don't look at me like that. I suppose you never went parking when you were a kid."

Rhonda could feel a blush creeping into her cheeks. "Well, if you must know, Mark and I got caught parking down at Storrs Lake one Saturday night. It was rather embarrassing. We weren't doing much other than making out, but I felt like we'd got caught doing the nasty in his car."

Jenny was still laughing when they got out of the car and walked over to the parking area.

"It doesn't look like this place is as well used as it was when I was in high school," she commented. "There's only one set of tire tracks and it looks like this was where the vehicle was parked."

Rhonda looked around and was surprised when she noticed what looked like a moccasin print in the sand covering the parking area. Next to it were several cigarette butts. Grabbing a pair of latex gloves, she carefully picked up the butts and put them in an evidence bag.

"That's strange," she commented. "These are hand rolled cigarettes. Who does that anymore?"

"How about someone who's smoking marijuana? Looks like a blunt to me."

"That could be, but being in cowboy country, it could also be someone who rolls their own smokes. Guess we won't know until we get the lab report back on this stuff."

Jenny placed a call to the office to have someone come out and get casts of the tire tracks. Even though they took plenty of pictures, they both agreed having plaster casts would be a good tool in finding the vehicle that made them.

By the time they got back to the office, it was time to call it a day. Even though they found out who the victim was and how the killer got away, they were still at square one in the investigation. They had no idea who killed Nancy or why they chose to do it at such a remote location, with such a primitive weapon.

Chapter Eight

The following morning, Rhonda went to the office with no high expectations of any evidence being gleaned from the yellow bug. She was more interested in seeing what if anything had been retrieved from the smashed cell phone.

Several glossy photos taken at various sites around the canyon were on her desk as soon as she arrived at work. Amongst them were photos like the one Nancy sent to Sara on Sunday. In the blown-up version the shadow was easier to make out. If she hadn't known better, she would have said it belonged to Johnny Depp in the character of Tonto.

"How in the hell did this guy get out of the park without being seen by someone? I looked around the area and I wouldn't have wanted to tackle getting out of there."

Jenny smiled. "I can tell you're not from this area. There are a lot of dyed in the wool hikers and climbers out here. I'm willing to bet there are a lot of people who could get in and out without going through the visitors' area. More than likely, they can make their way to other areas of the loop without being seen."

Rhonda looked through the pictures one more time. "So, what do we have here? The way I see it, our killer is a rock climbing, hiking enthusiast, Johnny Depp look alike, who is using primitive weapons."

"What do you mean our murderer is a Johnny Depp look alike?" Jenny questioned.

Rhonda picked out the picture with the shadow on the rock. "I haven't seen the movie, The Lone Ranger, but I have seen the trailers. This shadow looks like someone is wearing a headdress like the one in the movie. I don't want to think this is a Native American, but I do think it is someone who is trying to emulate the culture. I can't imagine the Native Americans I know dressing up like that to visit a national park."

"Oh, I see it now. It almost makes sense with the murder weapon. Were the tech people able to get anything else off the phone?"

After shuffling through the printed-out pages, Rhonda came to what she was looking for. There was a printout of the phone calls Nancy made recently as long as a text conversation just hours before her death.

Nancy: going out to red rock.

Dave: can't make it today.

Nancy: 2 bad – don't like to climb alone.

Dave: u should take some 1 with u.

Nancy: u r my last resort

Dave: b careful babe

"I think we need to talk to Sara and find out who Dave is. It sounds like he knew exactly where she was going but it's the last statement that bothers me. Why would he tell her to be careful?"

Jenny took a moment to look over the text message. "Out here you don't go hiking alone, especially in Red Rock. That's some treacherous terrain. I agree we need to find out who Dave is. I think it's time to call Sara in to ask her some questions."

Two hours later, Sara was in the interrogation room. Before they started questioning her about some of the numbers from Nancy's phone, as well as the identity of the man she'd been texting prior to her final trip to Red Rock Canyon, Rhonda assessed the young woman sitting across from her.

"Thank you so much for coming in to talk to us," Jenny began.

"I want to do anything I can to help you find Nancy's killer. I've heard from several of our friends, and we're all spooked. Nobody is going anywhere alone."

"I've got a listing of numbers from Nancy's phone," Rhonda said, handing the printed list to Sara. "Are there any of them you recognize?"

"Almost all of them. All but this one." She pointed at a number with a Las Vegas area code. "I can easily write down the names to correspond with the numbers."

"We'd appreciate all the help you can give us. Do you know this Dave who Nancy was texting prior to going out to the park?"

Sara pondered the printout for a moment. "She had to be getting desperate if she was texting Dave. Most of the numbers on her list were to friends we have in common from class. As for Dave, well they dated about a year ago and broke it off because he wanted more out of their relationship than Nancy was willing to give. As far as I know they hadn't been together much in the last six months. His name is Dave Remington and he's got a loft just off the strip down by the Palms. Nancy called him the poor little rich boy. Daddy bought the loft so Dave wouldn't have to live in one of the dorms with the rest of us peons."

Rhonda jotted down the location of Dave Remington and decided to have the young man brought into the office for questioning.

"What was so pressing that Nancy went out to the park by herself?"

"She's been working on a research paper for class based on the petroglyphs of the area. She's been out there several times but wanted one more trip before she finished the paper. It's due next week and I know she was anxious about one of the markings she wanted to study more closely. I told her if she waited until today, we could go out together and compare notes, but she was determined to get it done so she could spend today working on the paper."

After about an hour, Jenny thanked Sara for coming in and being so helpful.

"I've put a trace on that number Sara couldn't identify." Rhonda said. "In the meantime, let's see if we can find Mr. Remington."

~ * ~

Not being completely familiar with the area, Rhonda was more than willing to allow Jenny to do the driving. The way she maneuvered the busy Las Vegas streets was amazing.

"When I heard Mr. Remington lived in a loft, I had a feeling it would be this place. It's quite an exclusive building with a security guard and cameras all over the place."

Rhonda smiled as she recognized the building as the one where Tyson lived. Her relationship with him might work to her advantage if they couldn't gain access to the building.

She was pleased when the guard let them into the lobby area after Jenny held up her badge.

"How can I help you ladies?" the man asked, after getting a closer look at both of their identifications.

"We need to speak to one of your residents," Jenny replied. "We're hoping Mr. David Remington can give us some information on a case we're working on."

"I saw Mr. Remington leave about an hour ago."

"Could he have come back without you seeing him?" Rhonda questioned.

"If he'd taken his car I wouldn't have known, but he said he was meeting friends, and he wouldn't be back until much later. At the time I was impressed to think he wouldn't be going out on the town and driving. You know how young people are these days. Wouldn't want to have him get hurt or hurt someone else in a traffic accident. If you leave me your cards, I'll make certain he gets them so he can contact you."

Rhonda nodded. That was the one good thing about secure buildings. The security guards, at least, made certain the tenants received the business cards left by the police.

"I've often wondered what it would be like to live in a secure building. Somehow, I think I much prefer having my own home."

As soon as Rhonda said the words, she remembered the vandalism she'd had at her home in Wisconsin. If she'd been living in a secure building at the time it probably wouldn't have happened. That was the good part, but bad would be having someone know your every move.

Jenny fastened her seatbelt before answering. "I used to wonder about things like that too. Right after my divorce I was able to sublet an apartment in a building like this one. It was all right, but I thought it was very restricting. As soon as the lease was up, I went house hunting and found something I felt comfortable with."

In just one statement, Rhonda felt she'd learned some valuable information about her new partner.

~ * ~

By the time Rhonda got home from her first day at work she was more confused than ever. The body of the young woman had been identified and the grieving parents notified. There were still a lot of loose ends in this investigation, including the mysterious shadow depicted in the picture taken at the petroglyphs just before Nancy Callahan's murder.

If there hadn't been so much hype about the new Johnny Depp movie, The Lone Ranger, the shadow would have been confusing but it seemed to make sense. Could the killer be a Native American or a white man playing a part, much like Johnny Depp?

Mark met her at the door with a chilled glass of wine and a plate of cheese and crackers. "So, how was your first day at work?" he asked.

"Interesting. At least we identified the victim from yesterday. This is going to be a baffling case."

"What else is new? One thing in your favor is that none of the bad guys in this area know where you live. They don't know what you're capable of when you put your mind to it. That said, your bosses are in the dark about your abilities too. It might work in your favor."

Chapter Nine

Tuesday morning Rhonda was greeted by a message from Jenny saying she'd been contacted on her cell phone by David Remington, and he'd be coming into the office for an interview at nine thirty.

She'd just finished adding the appointment to the calendar on her phone when Jenny entered the office.

"I see you got my message. I honestly didn't expect to hear from this guy, but he proved me wrong."

David was not only on time, but early for the appointment he'd set with Jenny the night before. Although Rhonda remembered Sara referring to him as a 'poor little rich boy', she found him to be a well-spoken young man.

"Thank you for coming in," Jenny said when they sat across from David in the interrogation room.

Rhonda was more than willing to allow Jenny to take the lead in the interview, giving her a chance to see how her partner handled an interrogation. Being new to the department, she felt she needed to observe and adapt rather than pushing her way of doing things on her new colleagues.

"Is this about Nancy?" he asked.

"Yes. We were able to obtain the text messages from her phone and it seems as though you were one of the last people she contacted. Were the two of you lovers?"

David laughed at the question. "I wish. Nancy was a wonderful girl. We tried the boyfriend girlfriend thing, but it didn't work out. After having sex one time, we realized we were better friends than we were lovers. I considered her one of my best friends."

"Do you know anyone who would want to see her dead?"

"That's like asking who would want to kill the Easter Bunny or the Tooth Fairy. Everyone loved Nancy. I always worried when she went hiking on her own. I tried to talk her out of going out there on Sunday, but she assured me everything would be fine. She'd been researching all of the petroglyphs in the area for her class. Like she always said, what could possibly happen to me with all the tourists wandering around?"

"That's something that's been bothering us," Jenny probed. "How do you think the murderer could have gotten away without being seen by the tourists? My partner and I were out there on Sunday and there were a lot of people around."

Even though Rhonda and Jenny knew how the killer got away, she was anxious to hear what David had to say on the subject. Was it possible he knew about the road the park ranger told them about yesterday? She watched as David sat, as though deep in thought, for a moment.

"There is a back door," he finally said. "It's not much of a road and it's pretty treacherous, but it can be maneuvered. It's called Rocky Gap Road. It would be hard to get a vehicle back there, but it could be hiked. I used to sit in on a group who talked about all the back roads leading to things like the petroglyphs."

"Do you remember the name of the group?" Rhonda asked, her interest piqued.

"They called themselves the Society of the Arrow. Of course, all the guys who made up that group graduated a couple of years ago.'

"What did this group do?"

"They were a bunch of freaks. The one meeting I went to, they talked about how they worshiped the way the Native American's worshiped hundreds of years ago. They felt the petroglyphs were left by the Sky People; you know that stuff you see on that show Ancient Aliens. I thought it was a bunch of crap. After I went to a couple of meetings, I quit going."

"Do you remember the names of any of the people who belonged to this group?"

"The only names they ever used were ones that sounded as though they were all characters in a cheap western. You know they called themselves Running Deer and Charging Antelope, crazy stuff like that. They were too far out for me. I was happy studying geology and seeing the petroglyphs on occasion. I wasn't obsessed with them. When they wanted me to take a Native American name, I said thanks but no thanks. That's when they told me they were probably going to disband because they couldn't get any of the underclassmen to join them. That was a couple of years ago and I haven't heard anything about them since."

Rhonda jotted notes furiously. She needed to do a Google search for the Society of the Arrow. They sounded like persons of interest in this case.

~ * ~

The computer gave her quite a bit of information on the Society of the Arrow, but nothing recent. It seemed as though what David said about them disbanding two years earlier was true. The group had been active for many years on the UNLV campus, but from what she could ascertain, it was more of a secret society than anything else. Like David said, the names listed were Indian names rather than the true identities of the members of the society. The one name she did come across was Roger Racing Horse Jenkins. He was listed as the webmaster for the site.

"Did you find anything?" Jenny asked once she returned from the interrogation room.

Rhonda turned her laptop so Jenny could read the screen. "Does this name mean anything to you?"

"You're kidding, right? Roger Racing Horse Jenkins has a shop just off the strip. He sells Native American souvenirs, but the locals all have the feeling he gets most of them shipped in from China. There's nothing illegal about what he's doing, but unethical is something else. Do you think he's involved in this?"

"Probably not, but it's worth checking out his shop."

Rhonda finished up what she was doing, including marking the website as one of her favorites and went along with Jenny to the shop they'd talked about earlier. On the way to the backstreet shop, they stopped for lunch.

"When I come down to this area, I always like to do my lunch breaks on Fremont Street. I like the atmosphere and I enjoy eating at Binion's."

"You're kidding. Do you like all that noise?"

"You'll get used to it. I was born and raised around here. My dad has worked at Binion's for years. I always like to stop in whenever I can to see him in his element."

"What does he do?"

"He's worked in security for a long time. He says they're good people to work with and it's as close as he can get to police work. He was on the Metro force until he was involved in a shooting. It left him crippled up too much to stay on the force. That's when he landed his job at Binion's. He's been there ever since."

Rhonda followed Jenny into the noisy casino and over to the small restaurant area. After they ordered their salads and sat down, she saw a man in a wheelchair coming toward them.

"Hi there, baby girl, what brings you downtown?"

"I wanted you to meet my new partner, Dad. Rhonda Pohs. This is my dad, Matt Sims. I know what you're thinking, since my ex-husband and I didn't have kids, I took back my maiden name."

Rhonda fought the urge to get to her feet, knowing the action would possibly make Jenny's father ill at ease. Instead, she held out her hand. "It's a pleasure to meet you, Mr. Sims. I haven't been working with Jenny long, but I think we make for a good team."

"Have you got a minute to sit with us, Dad?" Jenny asked.

"I figured there was a reason you asked me to come over. Why don't we have your lunch brought back to my office? It's at least quiet there."

Rhonda smiled, convinced this was what Jenny planned all along. As she got up to follow Matt, she reached for her purse to pay for lunch.

"Don't," Jenny cautioned. "Dad runs a tab here. He'll be insulted if you attempt to pay for lunch. He's always been the guy who likes to treat everyone. You can join us when I take him out for dinner some evening. I know he gets lonely, so coming down here gives me a chance to see him and then make arrangements to get together again in the future."

"What about your mom?"

"She split right after Dad got hurt. She said she didn't want to play nursemaid for the rest of her life. I was a teenager then and I guess she figured I'd take good care of him as well as myself. Haven't heard from her since."

Rhonda bit back a sarcastic answer about anyone who would leave a man in a wheelchair and a teenager. It certainly didn't come as a surprise. She knew enough people who were just as uncaring.

Matt Sims' office was relatively large. Within minutes of arriving, the salads they'd ordered, along with three burgers and Styrofoam cups containing their drinks were delivered. "We only ordered salads," Rhonda protested.

"Sounds like sissy food to me," Matt replied. "You can't expect to do your best work eating rabbit food. Now you usually want some kind of information. What can I help you with?"

Jenny laughed. "You do get right to the point, don't you, Dad?"

"I have to. If I let you beat around the bush like you usually do, we could be here all afternoon and I only get a half an hour for lunch. So, what's up?"

"What do you know about Roger Racing Horse Jenkins?"

Matt nodded his head, as though the name struck a chord with him. "You need to know, he's a wanna be Indian if there ever was one. What's he gotten himself into now?"

"Nothing I can really talk about. We're looking into a group called the Society of the Arrow."

"I haven't heard that name in a while. I didn't know they were still around."

"From what I found on the Internet, they haven't been active for about two years, but it looks like Jenkins is maintaining their website," Rhonda replied.

"Makes sense. As much as he wants to be an Indian, he's always been a computer geek. I met him back in 2005. I was working on a case at the University, and he was a lot of help with the computer stuff. I never expected him to end up in that little hole in the wall shop of his."

Jenny changed the subject, and they talked about when Matt would be able to meet her for dinner and maybe a show. As though an alarm had been set, Matt said he had to get back to work exactly a half an hour after their food was delivered.

It didn't take long for Rhonda and Jenny to make their way to the Indian artifacts shop. As soon as they stepped in the door, Rhonda felt overwhelmed by the heavy scent of sage permeating the air.

"Welcome," a man said, coming from the back.

Rhonda assessed the man. He was in his mid-thirties and had his long brown hair hanging in braids down his back. He was dressed in buckskins and wore a beaded headband.

"Mr. Jenkins, I'm Jenny Sims."

"I recognize that name. You must be Matt's daughter. We worked together on one of his cases. I was sorry to hear he had to leave the force. How is he doing?"

Jenny made small talk about her father for a few minutes before getting to the reason for her visit. "I'm here on business," she finally said, producing her badge. "I'm wondering what you can tell us about the Society of the Arrow."

Roger's expression turned from cordial to a frown. "That's a defunct organization. I did their website, but they haven't been active in a couple of years. It's a shame no one is interested in the history of the native people of this area. At one time, they were a good group to belong to, but then turned into a bunch of radicals. I was glad to see them disband."

"You're still listed as webmaster for them," Rhonda probed.

"I've been the webmaster for them ever since college, but it doesn't mean much when there is nothing to update. It gives me more time for running my shop and keeping up my own website." He turned from them and went back to the counter to retrieve business cards with his website address as well as the information on the shop.

"Do you know if there are any of the former members of the group in the area?"

Roger shook his head. "Lloyd Charging Antelope Carpenter is a dealer at the Palms, and Steven Flying Arrow Anders lives in Reno. As for the others, I haven't had any contact with them in months."

Jenny thanked him for the information and asked him if he would be available to come into the office if they needed anything further from him. Once he said he'd be happy to be of help, they left the shop.

Rhonda breathed deeply of the somewhat fresh air. Even laced with diesel fuel and gas from the heavy traffic around the area, it was refreshing to not smell sage.

"That was quite the shop," she observed. "I've seen shops like his in Wisconsin, but they seemed to be more open than his."

"I think he does most of his business from his website, rather than walk in's."

"I gathered that. I'm anxious to get back to the office to check out his website and see if there's anything there we can use to solve this case."

Once they were back in the car Rhonda thought of something she saw in the shop. "Did you see that display of headdresses?"

"Can't say that I did. What are you getting at?"

"Way at the back of the shop there was quite a display of them. I wish I had taken some pictures, but I can't go back in and start snapping. There was one that reminded me of the elaborate one Johnny Depp wore in The Lone Ranger. That said, I think we need to find out who is buying those things from him."

"I see what you mean. It's possible our killer got his headdress there. I think we should run this past Karl and get his take on it. He can probably get us a warrant if Jenkins doesn't want to cooperate and give us his records."

By the time they returned to the office, Rhonda was more than ready to go home. Instead, she found not only a report on the butts they found at the pull off area where they saw the tire tracks but also what appeared to be a file on another case.

"What do you think this is?" Rhonda asked, picking up the file.

"I don't know, but I have a feeling it's something Karl thinks we need to see. For now, I'm more interested in this report."

Rhonda watched as her partner scrutinized the paper containing the results from the lab.

"Just as I thought," Jenny proclaimed. "We aren't looking for a cowboy rolling his own smoke. This guy is a verified pot head and he's using the good stuff too. They were even able to get DNA from the butt."

"Great. Now all we have to do is find a pothead who's willing to give up his DNA. How hard will that be in this city?"

Jenny laughed at Rhonda's comment.

Unable to control her curiosity any longer, Rhonda opened the file. To her horror, she saw a crime scene that reminded her of what she'd found at Red Rock Canyon on Sunday. The difference was the victim was male and had a war lance in his chest. On the stone wall above him was another set of petroglyphs.

"I see you found my gift," Karl said from the doorway of the cubical. "After I studied your pictures, I remembered this case. It went cold about eight years ago. We called it the petroglyph murder for years, but never got any leads."

"Did this take place in Red Rock Canyon?" Rhonda asked, her interest piqued.

"No. It took place down in Searchlight."

The word Searchlight resonated in Rhonda's head. "That's by where I live."

Karl smiled and winked slyly. "I know. Why do you think I gave this to you? I thought you might want to go out there and get a feel for this case tomorrow morning. Jenny lives in that area as well. You can get directions to get to her place and pick her up on your way to work."

"In other words, you think the doer in this cold case and ours could be one and the same. It could be interesting. I just hope our case doesn't go cold for eight years. I don't think I could take that for my first case working for Clark County."

"I do think they're one and the same. For some reason they left the area but have come back to the scene of their first crime."

Chapter Ten

Rhonda was surprised to learn Jenny lived less than five miles away from the house she and Mark had just moved into.

By seven the next morning, Rhonda pulled into Jenny's driveway and gave her a couple of beeps of her horn. It didn't take long for Jenny to come out looking more like someone ready for a day of hiking rather than a homicide detective.

Rhonda smiled, glad to see her own hiking gear wouldn't look out of place as they explored the area that had been the scene of a horrific murder eight years earlier.

Using Jenny's instructions, Rhonda drove fifteen and a half miles when Jenny said they needed to turn left onto an unnamed road. "This is Keyhole Access Road," Jenny informed her.

"Are you sure? There are no markings. I'm not even convinced this is a real road."

"Positive. I grew up in this area, remember. We'll stay on this road for almost six miles then turn onto 165. That will take us to Nelson and from there we'll be looking for Eldorado Valley Road. It's the last named road so we have to watch carefully for the intersection. It takes us through the barbwire fence at the white cattle guard with a 'designated roadway' sign. You can't miss it, it's the only road in the vicinity."

"Wow, I thought the cabin Mark's parents had in Wisconsin was remote. This is certainly out in the boonies."

Jenny laughed. "Out here we call it the desert. Karl left me a copy of the file he gave you last night. Since this is such an out of the way place, the murder wasn't reported right away. It wasn't until someone called into the station and left a message, they should send someone out here that anyone came out to investigate. They hung up before anyone could get a trace on the call or even get the informant's name. At the time, the detectives handling the case thought the informant was also the murderer."

"So, what happened to the original detectives who handled this one?" Rhonda inquired.

"Tom Spanton was killed in a car accident about three years ago and his partner Alex Meyers transferred to the state patrol in Colorado. Of course, that was before my time on the force, but Dad knew both of those guys. He said he got to thinking about our case after he reread the article in the paper. Dad also worked the case for a while, but it all led to dead ends."

"Does he think our friend Roger could be involved in this?"

"Dad doesn't know, but he is convinced the Society of the Arrow was somehow involved. They just couldn't prove it. At the time, they thought it was someone from the Native American community who was upset with the number of students and civilians out there studying the petroglyphs. I mean they are something of interest to everyone. All that hype about sky people and the ancients is certainly intriguing."

"I'll say it is. I remember going to a place called Cahokia Mounds with Mark one year on vacation."

"Cahokia Mounds? Never heard of it. Is it connected to the ancients?"

"You could say that. They were known as the Mississippians. Their village is just outside of St. Louis in Illinois. There's another village up by where we lived in Wisconsin, too. They were mound builders, and they must have had an extensive trade route. Unlike the people out here, they didn't leave a written language. I've always been intrigued by them. I guess that's why I was so excited about seeing the petroglyphs at Red Rock Canyon."

"The ancients have left us a tantalizing record of their existence and it's our duty to try to understand them. Unfortunately, now it seems like we have someone who is using them to carry out murders using ancient weaponry."

Rhonda agreed and continued driving down the desolate road. It gave her time to think about the two cases eight years apart. It certainly looked like they were related, but why pick such an isolated place as Keyhole Canyon for the first and as populated one as Red Rock Canyon for the second?

"What if this isn't the second killing?" Rhonda asked, hardly aware she voiced her concerns aloud.

"What are you getting at?" Jenny inquired.

"If this guy is a serial killer, why wait eight years between killings? It's possible this guy has been out of the area. You know, doing the same thing in other states. When we get back to the office I want to check with the authorities in Arizona as well as New Mexico. If he's obsessed with the petroglyphs, those would be good places to go."

The road led them to the barbwire fence at the cattle crossing, just like Jenny told her earlier. She was surprised to see two four-wheel drive vehicles parked at the side of the road.

"I didn't expect to have company out here."

"Get used to it, Rhonda. There are a lot of people out here who like to hike and study the petroglyphs. This is a great place for it, too."

"You sound like this is something you've done before."

"It is. When I was a kid, I had a friend whose dad was into this stuff. He used to take us with him on the weekends."

"So where is this guy now?"

"You aren't thinking Eddie or any of the other enthusiasts could be involved in this? Of course, we can rule Eddie out. He passed away from cancer about five years ago and my friend Marty is serving in the military. The last I heard he was stationed with the special forces in Germany."

"Let's face it, Jenny, in a case like this one everyone is a suspect until they're ruled out."

Rhonda parked next to one of the Jeeps and got out of her air-conditioned vehicle into the already rising temperature of the morning. As she looked around, she realized the hikers were nowhere to be found. Grabbing her water bottle she attached it to the belt of her shorts and followed Jenny along the trail leading into the rock-strewn wilderness.

Rhonda saw two older men on the trail ahead of them. "Is this a popular place for people to hike?"

"It is for diehard hikers and people into geology. I don't think many of your everyday tourists even know about it. I've been out here more than once but if you thought Red Rock was a treacherous hike, you're in for a reality check here. It's no wonder why the killer called the station to report the crime. It's doubtful the body would have been discovered before it was too badly decomposed to be recognizable. If I'm not mistaken our killer is an exhibitionist. He wants the world to see what he did and wonder why."

Considering the heat of the desert, Rhonda knew decomposition would have been a problem if the killer hadn't called the authorities.

"Haven't seen you girls out here before," one of the older men said once Rhonda and Jenny caught up with them.

"I'm new to the area," Rhonda admitted. "Do you come out here much?"

"I've been hiking out here for about ten years now," the second man said, holding out his hand. "I'm Jake Parker and this is my brother, Norm."

Rhonda smiled to herself. This was a great opening. "I'm Rhonda Pohs and this is my partner, Jenny Sims. We're Clark County detectives. Can I assume you knew about the murder that took place out here about eight years ago?"

Norm nodded sagely. "That was a bad one. It took a long time before we came back up here to hike. Too bad they never found the sick bastard that killed the kid. So why bring up something like that now?"

"We're investigating the murder that took place in Red Rock Canyon on Sunday. Luckily, someone recognized the similarities to the one that took place here," Jenny advised them.

"It's about time if you ask me, which you didn't," Jake stormed. "At the time I felt like the cops gave up too quickly."

"What do you mean?" Rhonda asked.

"If they'd taken the time to investigate the murder, you know ask those of us who know the canyon, we could have been of help. I told one officer about the religious ceremonies taking place out here, but he said it was irrelevant."

"What kind of ceremonies?" Rhonda probed.

"As I recall, there was a bunch of kids that came out from the university. They called themselves the Society of the Arrow. They'd come out here all dressed up like they were going to a pow-wow. I came upon 'em once and they were hootin' and hollerin'. When they saw me, they said if I knew what was good for me, I'd hightail it out of here. Since they had me outnumbered ten to one, I hot footed it back to my vehicle. Certainly didn't want to get mixed up with any of them."

"I had a similar run in with them," Norm added. "I think most of the people who come out here regularly could tell you the same story."

"Could you identify any of them?" Jenny questioned.

The two men exchanged glances that said more than any words. "Hell no," they said in unison.

It was Jake who continued. "They were all painted up like they were ready to go on the warpath. What I can tell you is, there wasn't a Native American in the bunch of them. They were all as white as you and me. The only thing I could see they were doing was mocking the real owners of this land."

For the second time in as many days, the name Society of the Arrow came up. For Rhonda it was like a flashing neon light leading back to Roger Racing Horse Jenkins. "Do you remember if they were armed?"

The two men paused for a moment before answering, as though trying to remember all the details of their encounter so many years ago.

"It was a while ago, but yes they were," Jake finally said. "As I recall, they were armed to the teeth. They had war lances, bows and arrows and knives. Weren't those knockoffs you see in the gift shops either. If I hadn't known better, I'd have thought I got thrown back about two hundred years."

Rhonda jotted notes fiercely, pleased to think she'd remembered to put a pad and pen in her backpack before leaving on the hike. Once she finished, she thanked the brothers for their help and took their contact information.

"Anything we could do to help," Norm said. "We're heading up to the petroglyphs. We'd be more than willing to have you accompany us. I didn't see the murder scene close up when it happened, but from the pictures in the paper I'm pretty sure we can show you exactly where it was."

His offer pleased Rhonda. Even though Jenny said she'd been out here before, it wouldn't hurt to have a guide who knew the area.

After about an hour of hiking, the rock walls containing the petroglyphs came into view. Although Rhonda photographed the ones she saw at Red Rock, she was even more awed by the sight of the ancient drawings. As many times as she'd seen documentaries on the History Channel, the video of them couldn't even begin to do them justice. Awe inspiring were the only words she could find to describe what graced the rock walls in front of her.

"I can see why anyone would want to have a religious experience here. I almost feel like worshiping the ancients myself."

Norm laughed at Rhonda's statement. "I know what you mean, but those kids tried to take things way too far. I have a feeling they were all high on drugs. There's always been a lot of talk about how the ancients smoked peyote to get high and commune with the spirits. It wouldn't surprise me if these kids were trying to emulate the ancients and totally immerse themselves in the culture."

Rhonda totally agreed. Although she felt drawn to the drawings on the rock face, she knew they had to get back to the office and decide what to do about Roger Racing Horse Jenkins and the rest of the young men involved in the Society of the Arrow. If any of them had been responsible for the killing, not only in Red Rock Canyon but also in Keyhole, why wait eight years between crimes?"

Along with her notes, Rhonda also had the contact information for both Jake and Norm. Their knowledge of not only the area but also the petroglyphs could be invaluable in their investigation.

~ * ~

"These guys sound like real groupies," Jenny said, after they stopped at Rhonda's home for a quick shower and a change of clothing. "How many members of the Society of the Arrow do you think are out there?"

"It's hard telling, but we'll have to look into this. I think we need to concentrate on the members of the society eight years ago. I'm convinced they're somehow involved in both of our murders. What I don't understand is why wait eight years between killings? I've read a lot about serial killers, and some of them do it for the thrill. In other words, there must have been other killings over the past eight years. Where else would they find petroglyphs since this seems to be the common denominator in both cases?"

"Something tells me we're going to spend the afternoon surfing the net to find other killings around the country that have connections to petroglyphs."

Rhonda laughed. "My dear husband may have saved us a bit of legwork. After going out to Red Rock Canyon, he's become obsessed with finding out about petroglyphs. He's even put together a folder on our computer to hold all the information. From what he's found, it looks like we're looking at a monumental job. Rock art exists all over the US, to say nothing of South and Central America. I think we need to ask for help on this one when we get back to the office."

Rhonda was right, it did turn out to be a big job. There had been murders in Pennsylvania, Maryland, Tennessee, New Mexico, Arizona, and California and those were just the first states to respond to her request for information. Up until now, the killer hadn't perpetuated more than one murder in each state, making the connection between all of them almost impossible.

In each of the murders, ancient weapons, like the ones used in Nevada, had been used. They included everything from knives and lances to war clubs, all depending on the area of the country where the murders took place."

"We know the where and the how, we just don't know who," Rhonda observed. "I think it's time we pay another visit to our friend Roger and see if he has anything more to tell us about the members of the Society of the Arrow."

Jenny agreed, but due to the lateness of the hour they decided to call it a day and make another visit to downtown Las Vegas the next morning.

Chapter Eleven

Since Roger's shop didn't open until eleven in the morning, Rhonda and Jenny spent the time sending emails to various law enforcement agencies around the country for any information they could get on the petroglyph murder that took place in their jurisdictions.

Knowing the information could be slow in coming in, they made their way down to Fremont Street and yet another meeting with Jenny's dad.

"I wanted to thank you for your help," Rhonda said once they were seated in Matt's office. "Can you tell me if you know how to get ahold of Alex Meyers?"

"I've got an address and other information for him back at the house. I'll be able to look it up when I get home tonight. Why do you want to talk to him?"

Jenny looked her dad in the eye and Rhonda knew telling him about the information given to the original officers that wasn't followed up on was going to be rough.

"Well, Dad, we went out to Keyhole yesterday and met up with some hikers. It seems they gave information to the detectives looking into the murder out there that was ignored. Remember us talking about the Society of the Arrow the other day?"

"Of course, I do. They were never on the radar with that case."

"Well, they should have been, or at least that's what Jake and Norm Parker seem to think. I want to know why Alex didn't think their information was credible. They certainly sounded credible to us. As a matter of fact, we're going to ask them to come in to give statements. Thank goodness there's no limit on prosecuting murderers."

"Don't be too hard on Alex until you talk to him. As I recall, he was in the same position you're in now. It was his first murder. Tom was the seasoned detective and the primary on the case. I was just one of the many deputies who helped out on the case, and I can tell you, it wasn't Alex who turned down help from the Parker brothers. Tom was a hardnosed detective, and he wasn't about to take information from a couple of hikers who probably didn't know squat, as he put it."

"You knew about this information and didn't say anything, Dad? How could you?"

"I knew bits and snatches about what was going on. When I talked to Alex about it, he said he'd been told to either go along with what Tom was saying or go back to driving a squad car chasing speeders. Back then you went along with what your superiors told you."

Rhonda remembered her stint with the Milton Police Department back in Wisconsin. There, she'd been the token woman cop and grief counselor. She, like Matt, did what she was told without question and was glad to have a job. It was easier to follow orders than to be out of work.

"The other day when we went to Roger Jenkins' shop, he mentioned a dealer over at the Palms by the name of Lloyd Carpenter. Do you know anything about him?"

Matt went silent for a moment as if contemplating the name she had just given him. "He worked here when he was in college. I think they offered him more money at the Palms and were able to work around his schedule for his day job."

"Just what is his day job?" Rhonda inquired.

"He's a researcher in the geology department over at the university. At least he was the last time I heard anything from him. That might be a good place for you to start looking for him."

Rhonda nodded. The best way to get information on the Society of the Arrow would be to talk to one of the former members.

Half an hour later Rhonda and Jenny were waiting to meet with Lloyd Carpenter at the University.

"What's a guy with his own office at the University doing dealing Blackjack?" Jenny inquired.

"It could be the University doesn't pay their researchers much money or it could be the guy did it in college and likes the extra money he can make by moon lighting."

"Mr. Carpenter will see you now," the secretary who left the office a few minutes before said.

Rhonda thanked her and, together with Jenny, entered what she'd mistakenly thought was an office. Instead, it was a large room with four young men all working on projects.

"Welcome to the 'think lab'," he greeted them, extending his hand. "I'm Lloyd Carpenter. How can I be of help to you?"

Rhonda and Jenny identified themselves and told him of their search for information on the Society of the Arrow.

"I'm sure you know I was a member of that group when I was a student here. For the first three years, it was a lot of fun dressing up in regalia and going to the area pow-wows. We did a lot of research into Native American cultures. That was the part I liked the most. By the time I was a senior, I could hardly wait to go to some of the rituals I'd been hearing about for the past three years."

"What kind of rituals" Jenny interjected.

"That's what I wanted to find out. It was all really hush-hush back then. I thought they would be reenacting the ceremonies of the ancestors. I went out with them on one of their excursions to Grapevine Canyon. We went there late one night and everything I thought would happen didn't. It turned out to be little more than a pot party, only these guys were smoking peyote. They were all dressed up like we did for the pow-wows, but they were also brandishing a lot of weapons and wearing war paint. That's when I left the group. When it was fun and games, I was all for it, but I didn't want anything to do with the drugs and everything else they were doing."

"Did you ever hear anything about someone being murdered by the petroglyphs in Keyhole?" Rhonda asked.

"Of course, I did. I've always lived in the area. At that time, I was eighteen years old and a senior in high school. It was all anyone could talk about. I think that's why I went into the field of study I did when I was in college. Do you think the Society of the Arrow could have been involved in that?"

Rhonda weighed her words carefully. "The name seems to keep popping up. We're actually looking for members of the group from eight years ago. With this killing in Red Rock Canyon, we're beginning to wonder if whoever is behind this could be a serial killer. We've been finding killings like the one in Keyhole and the one in Red Rock throughout the country."

The color seemed to drain from Lloyd's face, telling Rhonda he knew nothing about the killings that could be of help.

"I'm shocked to hear there might be someone from our group capable of something like that."

"Considering the first killing was before you joined the group, you probably don't know anyone who could have been involved. If you think of anything that could be of help, please feel free to contact either of us." Rhonda handed him both of their business cards.

"I think we shook him up," Jenny said once they were back in the car. "Is it possible he knows more than he's telling us?"

"It's possible, but what he does know is probably hearsay rather than personal knowledge. It sounds like going to one of their rituals was enough to scare him off. Like he said, it was fun playing Indian at the pow-wows but the drugs and talk of violence were too much for him."

"Maybe we can get more information from Roger."

Rhonda and Jenny were both surprised to find the shop closed. The sign in the window said there had been an emergency and the shop would be closed indefinitely. The website was listed at the bottom of the sign along with an email address, but no phone number where he could be reached if someone really wanted to buy any of his artifacts.

"Where do we go now?" Jenny asked, after writing down the website as well as the email address.

"I think we go back to the University. If the Society of the Arrow was a club at the school, they should have membership lists available. According to Lloyd, only the seniors could take part in the rituals, therefore, the seniors in this organization eight years ago would be the ones to target."

~ * ~

The University proved to be a great place to do their research. Not only did they have the names of the members of the Society of the Arrow from eight years earlier, they also had records going back over twenty plus years to the beginning of the organization. The one name to pop up through many of the lists was Roger Jenkins. It was evident he was very active from the time he started college until long after his graduation thirteen years ago.

"Do you know the extent of Mr. Jenkins' involvement with the group?"

The library attendant stood mute for a moment. "I honestly don't know his involvement, other than he's listed as the webmaster for the website and has been for many years. According to our records he graduated with the class of 2000 and joined the group in 1996, about six years after they were founded in 1990. The records also indicate the group disbanded two years ago, but the website has been active ever since it was set up in 1996."

Rhonda scanned through the information, including the names of the seniors listed for the year 2014 and 2015. "By any chance do you have contact information for Mr. Jenkins other than his website and email?"

The young man shuffled through several sheets of paper until at last he wrote down a cell phone along with an address in Mesquite, Nevada.

"Thank you for all this information. You've been a big help."

Once back at the office, Rhonda made copies of the two lists of former members of Society of the Arrow and gave them to Jenny. "You're the native here, do you have any idea who any of these people are?"

Jenny took a minute to look over the lists. "This is interesting," she said, when she finished reading through them. "It says here that in 2014 Tom Spanton's son, George, who was also known as Wounded Beaver, was a member of the group. I'm surprised he was even given the case, unless his lieutenant didn't know of George's involvement."

"It could be because no one associated the group with the murder out at Keyhole. If Spanton didn't want to listen to what the Parker brothers had to say, there had to be a reason. It's possible he was privy to information about the group he didn't want made public. Who else is on the list?"

"Let's see. There's a listing for Darrel Hunting Hawk Williams, Alan Fighting Bear Knilans and Joseph War Lance Roberts. I don't recognize any of those names. I doubt they're even living in the area anymore. Of course, Dr. Bob Soaring Eagle Burton is also listed."

Chapter Twelve

It wasn't difficult to locate George Spanton as he worked security at the Palms.

"What is it with the guys from this society working at the Palms?" Jenny asked.

"I don't know, but Lloyd did say he worked there while he was going to school and continued working on the weekends to supplement his current income. I doubt if one has anything to do with the other. According to the information we got from the University, George has a BA in Law Enforcement. It sounds like he wanted to follow in Daddy's footsteps. It will be interesting to find out what he has to say."

They were in luck and found George working when they arrived at the Palms. In comparison to Matt's cluttered office at Binion's, George's office was clutter free as though he did very little work there.

"It's a pleasure to meet you, Detectives," he said as he ushered them into the office. "What can I do for you?"

"We're investigating the murder that took place on Sunday at Red Rock Canyon," Rhonda began. "In doing so we came across a cold case that took place out at Keyhole about eight years ago. In our investigation we came across the Society of the Arrow. According to our records, you were a member of that group when you were in college. Is there anything you can tell us about them?"

"Yes, I was a member of the group, but it was little more than a social club that studied Native American cultures."

"Studied?" Jenny's statement came out as a question. "I heard you attended pow-wows dressed in regalia as well as participated in religious rituals. What can you tell me about them?"

"Ah…there were reenactments of events that took place in sacred areas. As for the regalia, it was all part of the research we did. We were lucky that a former member gave us a discount on it at his shop."

"Are you talking about Roger Jenkins?"

"You know I am. He's been not only the webmaster of our site but also a benefactor to the group for years."

"Did you know when your father investigated the murder at Keyhole eight years ago, he dismissed some information pertinent to the case."

George became fidgety. "What kind of information? I can't believe my father would have done anything like that."

"From what we've learned, he was told about the rituals being performed by the Society of the Arrow and the threats they were making against the people who reported it to him. They were dismissed as nonsense, but they were enough to make us sit up and take notice."

"Just what fool is making accusations? I told you; the Society of the Arrow was a social group. Nothing more. If you don't believe me, talk to Roger. He knows what we were."

"Maybe he does, but his shop is closed indefinitely."

George's attitude changed almost instantly. Either he didn't know about the shop being closed, or there were things he wasn't telling them. If that were the case it was possible he didn't plan to divulge the information any time soon.

"I don't think there's anything else I can tell you ladies. If you'll excuse me, I've got work to do. I have your cards, so if I think of anything I'll call you."

Rhonda thanked George for his time and, with Jenny, left the hotel. "I think we've been dismissed. There's something strange about George, something he doesn't want us to know. I think we need to go back to the cold case file and see what we can come up with. I'm sure it holds the clue as to who our serial killer is."

~ * ~

"I think I've found something," Jenny said, as they poured over the file yet another time.

"What?" Rhonda questioned.

"The victim of the Keyhole killing was Gerald Kaiser. All the report says is that he was a sophomore at UNLV studying geology. I also found he was a member of the Society of the Arrow. Do you think the first killing could have been part of an initiation for the group?"

"It's possible. I wish I'd get answers to some of those emails I sent out this morning. It would be interesting to see if any of them mention the Society of the Arrow. It could be it's not just a local group."

As if on cue Rhonda's computer beeped, indicating an incoming email. "Let's hope this is the answer to our problem," Rhonda said as soon as she opened the internet to look at her inbox.

The incoming email was from Pennsylvania regarding the murder in their area. Before she could even open it another one from New Mexico was immediately followed by one from Arizona. Each of their murders closely resembled the two sitting on Rhonda's desk. Unfortunately, there was no mention of the Society of the Arrow. It was entirely possible the name never came up in any of the investigations. If Rhonda hadn't stumbled on it in connection with Nancy's murder, she wouldn't have linked it to the cold case in Keyhole.

"Here's something else," Jenny said, breaking into Rhonda's thoughts. "At the time of the murder, Gerald Kaiser's family lived in Boulder City. Do you think they might still live there?"

"It's worth a try. Hopefully they have some more information on their son than the report we have from the responding detectives."

~ * ~

Rhonda was relieved to find Gerald's parents still lived in Boulder City. After making a call they learned both parents worked but would be home after four. The timing worked out well, since they'd be able to stop by and interview the parents on their way home.

Ann Kaiser was young looking; a fifty-something woman with short auburn hair. Her husband, Bill, looked to be older than her, but of course it was entirely possible Ann dyed her hair while Bill didn't take the time to do anything so vain.

"We didn't think anyone was interested in Jerry's murder," Bill said, sarcasm dripping with every word. "I mean, it's been eight years, and no one has ever been arrested."

"I'm sure you read about the murder last Sunday in Red Rock Canyon. We caught that case and then were handed your son's case because of the similarities. We were wondering what your son might have said about an organization he belonged to called the Society of the Arrow."

"Jerry didn't tell us much about what went on at college. He did mention the Society of the Arrow and how through it he was able to study the Native American culture. He was always interested in it. He said they would be more tolerant of him."

"What do you mean by that?" Jenny asked.

"He loved to watch that movie Little Big Man, you know the one with Dustin Hoffman. Somehow, he got the idea the Indians revered people who were different."

"For god's sake, Ann, it's all right to say the word. Our son was gay. I think he joined that group because it was a macho thing to do. One thing Jerry wasn't was macho. I told him there was no shame in being different, but he always wanted to fit in. Well, he's been dead and in the grave for eight years now and no one gives a flying fuck whether he was gay or straight."

"Did Jerry ever say if he had problems with the members of the Society of the Arrow?" Rhonda asked.

"Hell no. He was the happiest he'd been in years. He loved dressing up and going to the pow-wows. He liked to ask questions of the participants and get information about the culture. I told him it was a waste of time, but he said he didn't care. He wanted to make his mark on the world and do something that people would remember for years to come. All he managed to do was get killed. He certainly didn't change the world, did he?"

Ann wept openly at her husband's tirade. It was evident this wasn't the first time he'd bad mouthed their son.

"It doesn't matter," Ann finally managed to say. "Nothing matters other than the fact our son is dead. As far as we know no one knows who killed him or why they did it. Thank goodness we have two other kids who are leading normal lives."

"Were your children close to Jerry?" Rhonda probed.

"Mac is Jerry's twin brother. I guess you'd say they were close, but the gay thing was hard for him to accept, considering Mac is in the Marines. As for Patsy, she's married and living in Seattle with her husband and kids. I don't think she ever actually thought Jerry was gay and with his murder he became a martyr in her eyes. It was easier to accept the fact her brother was murdered than to admit that he was gay."

Rhonda and Jenny both left their cards with the Kaisers and told them if they thought of anything that might be of help to give them a call.

"Yet another twist in this case," Jenny commented. "Do you think the fact Jerry was gay had anything to do with why he was murdered?"

"I think it had a lot to do with it. What I want to know is what it has to do with Nancy's death? I'm beginning to wonder if she might have stumbled onto something about this case."

"I don't know about that. My guess is she interrupted something and paid for her mistake with her life. It could have easily been Mr. and Mrs. Johnson or you and Mark who came upon our killer."

Rhonda agreed with what Jenny just said. It was possible Nancy was the only innocent victim in this whole mess.

~ * ~

Once back at the office, Rhonda checked her email. She found responses from Pennsylvania, New Mexico and California, all describing murders that matched the ones they were now investigating.

"By the dates of these murders, I can see why we haven't had a murder in this area in the past eight years. If it's the same guy he's been busy. Let's see there was one in California, two in New Mexico and three in Pennsylvania. It looks like he started out small and has increased. We still have some more states to hear from, but it seems like he's come full circle and returned to his home and his first killing ground."

"How were the other murders done?" Jenny asked.

"Let's see. It seems like they were all done with ancient weapons. There was one with a war club in Pennsylvania. The other ones were with stone knives, war lances, and bows and arrows. They have to be connected, but what I can't understand is why use such outdated weapons?"

"Whoever is behind this has to be very knowledgeable about the ancient cultures. He's either an activist or one sick son of a bitch."

"Could it be a woman who's behind this?"

Jenny laughed at the suggestion. "I doubt it. I studied the ancient cultures and I do know in many of the tribes women were forbidden to touch the weapons. Did you take a good look at the membership lists for the Society of the Arrow? There's not a woman on any of those lists. Being such a male chauvinist group, I doubt any woman would be welcomed."

"Do you think that's why Nancy was targeted? It could be possible our killer could have known she was studying the petroglyphs and didn't approve of it."

"If that's the case, why didn't he strike when some of the other female students went out to see the same things?"

"How many of them went out there alone? I doubt you'll find many who would want to be hiking without a partner. How many times have you gone hiking by yourself?"

Jenny thought for a moment. "I was always told never to hike alone in case something happened. If you're by yourself, you're asking for trouble in case of an accident."

Rhonda agreed. From all the information she'd gathered on Nancy it was evident she'd tried her best to get someone to go out to Red Rock with her, but whatever it was she needed to research was important enough for her to go by herself even though it wasn't recommended.

Chapter Thirteen

Rhonda reviewed all the information regarding the case. What she really wanted was to get into Roger's shop, but with him out of town indefinitely, there was no way she would ever get inside until he returned to Las Vegas. In her opinion, the Stone Age weapons used in both the murders she was investigating could have easily come from him.

"You've got another body," Karl said as he entered her cubicle.

"What do you mean I've got a body?"

"We got a call from the office out at Valley of Fire that they found a body at Mouse's Tank."

"Where?" Rhonda asked, bewildered by the strange name given to the location.

Jenny laughed. "We have to get you acquainted with the area PDQ. Mouse was an Indian who supposedly stole from the whites in the area. His hideout was in the Valley of Fire in a natural depression that retained the rainwater. That was where they captured him and from then on it was called Mouse's Tank. There are a lot of petroglyphs there and it's quite a tourist area, just like where the first murder took place in Red Rock Canyon. Of course, it's harder to get to."

"Harder than that rock strewn path leading to the ones in Red Rock?"

"Well, there aren't a lot of rocks in that area, but it's filled with silicon sand. It makes hiking difficult but not impossible. They do say if you've had any joint replacements you shouldn't try hiking there. Myself, I enjoy it."

Rhonda shook her head. She knew there was a lot to learn about the area she now called home. "You said there was another murder. How do you know it's linked to the two we already have?"

"First," Karl began, "is the location. The petroglyphs have played a part in the first two murders and this one doesn't seem to be any different. The second is the murder weapon. We have to check things out but the people at the park have told me this victim was killed with a bow and arrow. Is that enough of a link for you?"

"It certainly is, especially with the information we've been getting from some of the other states with petroglyphs. I got another email about three murders in Arizona. This guy is prolific. I wish I knew what his agenda is."

"Maybe this murder will be a break in the case, but we won't know unless you girls shag your asses out to Valley of Fire and see what they have out there. They said they wouldn't remove the body until you get out there to investigate."

Karl winked broadly at them and tossed the keys to one of the unmarked vehicles in Jenny's direction. The friendly gesture on Karl's part put Rhonda at ease. She'd worked with and for some pretty hardnosed guys in the past and Karl seemed to be more like a regular guy than some of the others.

"What do you think we'll find out there?" Jenny asked as they drove out toward the park.

"I can't even venture a guess. I've been reading the notes on the out of state murders. The majority of them were males and all of them were college students. I'd hate to think of another young person losing their life to this monster."

"Why do you call him a monster? Couldn't he be like Ted Bundy or any of the other serial killers you hear about?"

Rhonda rolled her eyes. "All serial killers are monsters, even if they look like the average guy on the street. They've got to have a screw loose to do something like that in the first place."

"I guess you're right."

When they finally arrived at the park, Rhonda was almost overwhelmed by the beauty of the rock formations that greeted her. As much as she wanted to investigate the marvels of the park, she knew they had a murder to investigate and with the heat of the day getting ready to set in, they had no time to waste.

At the parking area for Mouse's Tank, Rhonda saw several park rangers along with county sheriff's deputies. "I'm Detective Pohs and this is my partner, Detective Sims. Can you take us to where they found the body?"

The deputy nodded. "I hope you're prepared to hike to get there," the young man said, looking down at Rhonda's hiking boots. "It's not an easy trek."

"So I've been told," Rhonda responded. "I think we're up to it. What can you tell me about this murder?"

"Not much. One of the rangers found the body this morning. The coroner said it probably happened sometime last evening. We found a campsite not far from where we found the body. It looks like this guy was camping out here or at least trying to camp out here. If anyone had caught him camping they would have informed him to move to the campsites or leave the park. He couldn't have been there very long, or he would have been spotted."

Rhonda was anxious to see the murder scene and followed the deputy up the trail to where a body bag obscured the body from view. "Can I see the body?" she asked. The coroner nodded and unzipped the bag. She certainly wasn't prepared for what she saw.

"Oh my god," Jenny gasped, "that's Roger."

Rhonda stared, transfixed for a moment by the bloodstain over his heart along with the hole in his shirt. "We were told he was killed with an arrow. Where is it?"

"I removed it," the coroner said. "We have plenty of pictures of him with the arrow in his chest and so I decided it was better to take it out to fit him into the bag. I'm sure the deputies have the arrow in their evidence bag."

Rhonda knew the coroner made sense and the pictures would give her a good idea of what happened during Roger's last moments of life, but she wished she'd seen the pristine scene for herself.

As the coroner did the final preparations to remove the body, Rhonda turned her attention to the deputy she spoke with earlier. "Can I see the arrow?"

The young deputy agreed and produced the evidence bag containing the murder weapon. Just from the man's attitude, Rhonda could tell he wished he was working with a man rather than two women.

Well, that's just too bad. I'm the primary on this case and Jenny is my partner. If he gives me any chauvinistic lip, I'm afraid I might tell him a thing or two.

The shaft of the arrow reminded Rhonda of ones she'd seen at Roger's shop as well as in several museums she visited in Wisconsin. Although the point was fashioned out of stone, it had been chiseled to a sharp point, much like those she knew bow hunters used for deer hunting back home.

"Do you know who makes arrows like this anymore?'

"You'd have to stop at one of the shops that sell Indian artifacts either in Mesquite or Las Vegas."

"I didn't know there was a shop in Mesquite," Jenny commented. "Do you know who runs it?"

"I thought everyone knew about it. It belongs to the guy who owns the shop in downtown Las Vegas."

Rhonda thought the comment was ironic, because the owner of not one but two Indian artifacts shops with a connection to the Society of the Arrow was being transported to the coroner's vehicle in a body bag. At first, she didn't think she would have to look much further than the shop Roger ran in downtown Las Vegas to get the answers she needed. Now the information about the shop in Mesquite changed everything.

"Where did you say the campsite was?" Jenny asked.

The deputy showed them to the site tucked away against the red rocks that filled the area. It could hardly be called a campsite, though. All Rhonda could see was a sleeping bag and a duffle bag. If Roger hiked in he certainly wasn't prepared to go camping. As far as Rhonda could tell, Roger wasn't planning to spend more than the night at Mouse's Tank, since he had no food in the duffle bag or utensils to cook any.

"I don't see anything here that could give us a clue," Rhonda commented. "I think it's best if we get back to Vegas and see if we can find anything in Roger Jenkins' shop."

"Don't forget the shop in Mesquite. I think we should investigate there first, since it's closer."

"We'll have to get a warrant for both shops. It's best if we start in Las Vegas."

"Whose shop?" the deputy asked, interrupting their conversation.

It took all the restraint Rhonda could muster not to verbally strike out at the man.

"It appears you weren't listening when we looked at the body," Jenny said, her voice sounding much calmer than anything Rhonda could have achieved at this point. "The victim is Roger Racing Horse Jenkins, the owner of a small Indian artifact shop in downtown Las Vegas, as well as the one in Mesquite. We're investigating at least two other murders in this area that are similar to this one. Thank you for all your help here. If we need any further information from you, we'll be in touch."

Once they were back on the highway heading toward Vegas, Rhonda started to laugh. "It's no wonder they put the two of us together as partners."

"What do you mean?"

"I don't think I could have been as diplomatic as you were back there. I wanted to pop that deputy. The look on his face when you told him who the victim was. He certainly couldn't have been so out of it he didn't hear us talking about Roger when we first got here."

"I've run into him before."

"Do you know him?"

"His name is Pete Winker, and we went to the academy together. When I made detective, he was pissed to the max. His comment was that I brown nosed my way into the position. Well, he couldn't be more wrong. I worked my tail off to get where I am today. Pete's idea of being an officer on the force is riding around in a squad car and picking up speeders out on the highway. I wanted more out of my career, and he resents it."

"Well, that certainly explains his attitude today. I sensed it as soon as he saw who we were. I remember being treated like that on my first job in law enforcement. After I solved the first murder, I was assigned the attitude changed. That's when I took my first job as a homicide detective with the county sheriff's department. I've enjoyed it ever since. I think the two of us are a lot alike in that department."

Before leaving the park, Rhonda placed a call to Karl. Unfortunately, she only got his voice mail. "If you haven't gotten a warrant for Roger's shop yet, get one for his shop in Mesquite as well."

By the time they returned to the office, Karl had gotten a warrant to search both of Roger's shops. "What did you find out at the park?"

"The victim is Roger Jenkins. That's why I called and asked you to get a warrant for the shop in Mesquite."

"You're kidding. I didn't hear anything about that. Did you call it in to me?"

"No," Rhonda said, feeling a bit like a chastised child. "We were told the report had been made by the deputy at the scene, Pete Winker."

"I got a report on the killing from him but not the identity of the victim.

Why don't you tell me what you saw out there?"

Rhonda reported on everything from the illegal campsite to the ancient murder weapon. "I don't think I've ever seen such a sharp point on an arrowhead, other than at Cahokia Mounds down by St. Louis. Those people knew how to make arrowheads. Whoever made the one used on Roger was a real craftsman. I'm hoping we can get a line on his vendors and see where something like this came from."

"How are we going to get into the locked door?" Jenny asked.

"We'll check at the morgue and see if by any chance they found keys on the body," Karl suggested. "That would be a godsend. I'd certainly hate to have to break down the door just to get inside a dead man's shop."

"What about the shop in Mesquite?" Rhonda asked.

"You girls take the one here in town. I'll send another team out to Mesquite and see what we can find there. I'm not sure I want any of the deputies securing the things there."

~ * ~

Rhonda was pleased when the coroner handed over the keys he'd found on Roger's body. Along with keys for the car Rhonda was sure had been parked somewhere at the park, they found a ring loaded with keys to try to open not only the shop but also Roger's apartment and at least three keys to lock boxes at three different banks in the area of his shop.

Walking into the deserted shop gave Rhonda an eerie feeling. Headdresses and regalia hung in the back of the shop where people could shop for clothing. In the front of the shop were the herbs, with the weaponry sandwiched between the two areas. When she'd been here before, the scent of sage was almost overwhelming. Today the shop smelled like a mixture of the herbs that had once been burned here and a musty scent from the clothing made from animal hides.

"Can we open some windows?" Jenny asked after experiencing a sneezing fit.

"I would if I could find them," Rhonda replied, stifling her own sneeze. "I thought the smell of the sage was bad, but the mixture of all the odors is absolutely overpowering. How about you look to see if you can open the back door and I'll prop open the front. At least we can get a cross breeze, if there is any breeze out there."

"Look at these arrows," Jenny said after opening the front door. "They look just like the one that killed Roger."

Rhonda hurried to the middle of the shop to look at the display of arrows. "How ironic that he would sell his killer the weapon that took his life. Oh, look at this, here's a war lance like the one that was used in Keyhole and a knife like the one used to kill Nancy."

"I know. I saw a war club over there as well as some tomahawks. My god, he has enough weapons here to kill just about everyone in Las Vegas with some left over."

"What I want to find is his sales records. Someone is buying this stuff that they're using for these killings. I need to find out who this stuff is being shipped to."

"I want to know what's in the safety deposit boxes at the banks."

Rhonda also wondered about the safety deposit boxes, but there was so much to go through here at the store, a trip to the bank was going to have to wait until everything here could be secured and taken to the office so it could be analyzed.

"Stay right where you are."

Rhonda turned at the sound of a man's voice coming from the doorway of the shop. To her shock, the man was holding a shotgun pointed directly at her. "We're…"

"I know what you are. You've broken into Roger's shop, and I won't let you get away with it. Stay right where you are, I've called 911 and the cops will be here to arrest you."

"But…" Jenny's words were cut short by the sound of sirens screaming in from at least two if not three directions all at the same time.

To Rhonda it seemed as though several officers of Las Vegas Metro materialized almost out of nowhere. "Put your hands in the air," the first officer to enter the shop, gun drawn, ordered.

"They broke in here, officer. Roger asked me to keep an eye on his shop while he was on vacation. I saw the door open and knew Roger wouldn't be back until the end of the week. I grabbed my gun right away and came over. I was right, I found these women ransacking the shop."

Rhonda obediently put her hands behind her back and allowed the officer to handcuff her. From the corner of her eye she saw Jenny starting to protest.

"Just do as they say, Jenny. We can straighten this all out."

"I hope so," Jenny said, putting her hands behind her back.

"Now, who are you?" the officer demanded.

"I'm Detective Rhonda Pohs of the Clark County Sheriff's office and this is my partner, Jennifer Sims."

"Can you prove that?"

"Of course I can." Rhonda nodded toward her purse with her badge pinned to the outside flap.

The officer picked it up, checked out the shiny new badge then looked inside for other identification.

"A Wisconsin driver's license?" he questioned.

Rhonda cringed. She wished she had applied for her Nevada driver's license the first week they were in town instead of putting everything off until just before she got hired in Clark County. She had the paper copy, but it was in a different compartment of her wallet.

"I'm waiting for my Nevada license to arrive. We only moved here about three weeks ago. If you don't believe me, call my boss, Karl Brannigan."

"If this shop is closed because the owner is on vacation, what are you doing here?"

"We're working on an ongoing investigation. We do have a warrant, but this morning Mr. Jenkins, the owner of this shop, was found murdered out at Valley of Fire. We're searching for clues as to who might have wanted the man dead."

From the doorway, she heard an audible gasp from the man who held them at gunpoint. She hadn't wanted the news of Roger's murder to come out this way, but in order not to be arrested, she had to tell them the truth in the matter.

The officer left Rhonda and Jenny alone, still handcuffed, as they contacted Clark County to verify their identification.

"Are we in deep shit here?" Jenny whispered.

"As soon as they get in touch with Karl, they'll find out who we are and release us."

"I'm sorry, Detective," the officer said, as he unlocked the cuffs, freeing Rhonda. "Your story checks out. Is there any help we can get for you, since this shop is in the city?"

"We could use some manpower. There are several things from the shop we need to take into evidence and some lock boxes we need to get access to."

"I-I'm sorry, Detective," the neighbor who first interrupted them said.

"Don't be," Rhonda assured him. "You should be commended for your vigilance. I wish all neighbors were as watchful for others as you. I'm sure if Roger were still alive, he would thank you himself."

Chapter Fourteen

"Just what the hell was going on out there?" Karl demanded once they arrived back at the office.

"A concerned citizen called Metro because he saw someone in Roger's shop." Rhonda explained. "I can't blame him, as a matter of fact I told him he did the right thing. The problem came when he wouldn't give us a chance to identify ourselves."

"Why in the hell didn't you have your paper copy of your license where it could be found?"

"It was there, it's just that they picked out the Wisconsin license first. They pulled it out later but by then the damage was done. Everything turned out all right. They even helped us get all the stuff we needed out of the shop and Roger's apartment down to the CSI department."

"So what did you get out of the apartment and shop?"

Jenny was quick to answer Karl's question. "There were three laptop computers in the apartment and another two in the shop along with a desktop. We also brought in his files along with several of the weapons like the ones that were used in the murders. My god, that man had enough weapons in his store to arm every Indian who ever fought in the Indian wars, including The Little Bighorn. He certainly wasn't making his money from selling the herbs and jewelry he kept in the front of the shop. Most of that stuff was junk, a lot of it came from China."

"Are you saying the money makers were the weapons?"

"They had to be. Those things are so original, they had to be made by Native American craftsmen. I just wonder if they ever thought they would be used in such horrific ways."

Karl ran his fingers through his hair as he appeared to contemplate what Jenny had just said. "Do we know who he gets this stuff from?"

"Not yet," Rhonda said. "I'm sure once we go through the files, we can find the craftsmen. It's going to be a lot of work to find the information. You have no idea how much information there is in those files. He had four cabinets each with four drawers packed full of paperwork. With all the computers he had, I can't believe he was still dealing with so much paper."

Rhonda knew the job of finding out about Roger's dealing would be overwhelming. She'd seen the amount of paperwork, not to mention the information contained on all of the computers. Of course none of it was as interesting as what they'd found in the safe deposit boxes.

"The stuff in the shop and apartment is overwhelming, but what we found in the safe deposit boxes came as a shock. Each of the boxes were the largest ones that could have been rented. Each of them contained a lot of money. Until it can all be counted, we won't know how much there is, but my guess is each one contained at least a half a million dollars. Not only that, there was some jewelry, not the junk stuff from his shop, but real silver and turquoise. We have to get it appraised, but if I don't miss my guess, it's worth almost as much if not more than the entire inventory of the shop. Some of that stuff was antique, pieces that should have been in a Native American museum."

"It sounds like you've got enough information to go through to keep you two busy for weeks," Karl said. "Unfortunately, we still have a serial killer out there, making everyone who visits the petroglyphs, not only in this area but anywhere else in the country, in danger."

"So," Rhonda began, "what did they find in Mesquite?"

"Not as much as you did, but they did bring back some paper files along with another two computers. It looked as though most of the stuff in the shop was cheap knock offs. The back room was interesting though. The detectives said it looked like a workshop to make artifact replicas."

The thought of Roger making the artifacts himself made Rhonda sick to her stomach. After the one brief meeting she'd had with the now deceased Roger Jenkins, she didn't think he had the expertise to fashion such elaborate weapons. He was a computer geek and nothing more.

~ * ~

"I've been listening to the news," Mark greeted Rhonda when she finally got home for the night. "It sounds like you're in the middle of a real humdinger this time."

"Oh honey, you don't know the half of it. We're getting emails from cold cases all over the country. Whoever is behind these killings has been a very busy boy. So far, we have at least twenty cases we can attribute to the same killer."

Mark enfolded Rhonda in his arms, and she could feel the tension of the past few days begin to drain from her body.

"Come on out to the patio and have a glass of wine. I've got dinner already on the table out there. I thought you might need something special tonight."

Rhonda made her way out to the patio and smiled at the shrimp cocktail sitting next to a glass of white wine. If Mark ran true to form, she knew she could expect a glass of red wine with a perfectly grilled steak to go along with it as the entree.

"You do know how to pamper me," she said, as she put her arms around his neck and gave him a kiss.

They'd just finished their dinner when Rhonda's cell phone rang. "You could ignore it, you know." Mark suggested.

She glanced at the caller ID. "I don't think so. This call is from Phil, back in Wisconsin. I don't want to talk to anyone tonight, but I feel I need to get his advice on this one."

"Hi Partner," Phil greeted her. "I was watching the six o'clock news and heard your name mentioned. What's going on out there?"

Rhonda relaxed, even though Phil was no longer her partner, she felt the need to get his advice about this case. He was far enough away he wouldn't be able to do anything to jeopardize her case. She glanced at her watch. Since it was eight o'clock here, she knew it was ten in Wisconsin. Once Mark went into the house, she bared her soul to her former partner.

"I'm in a real mess out here, Phil. I've got a murderer out there with more bodies than I care to think about that I can pin on him."

"I think you've got more bodies than you think. About six years ago I had a friend working up in Northern Wisconsin. They had a murder that sounds a lot like the ones you're dealing with. They arrested a young Indian kid for it, made the accusations stick, too, but the kid kept claiming he's innocent. I checked with my friend after I heard about you on the news, and he said the kid is still trying to get a new trial. I told my friend I'd get your fax number at work so he can send you what he has on this case in the morning."

Rhonda took a mental count of the number of years and knew it could have been one of the first murders in this case. It certainly predated the ones on the east coast as well as the ones in New Mexico, Arizona and California. The only older case she had on her books was the one at Keyhole.

"Do you have any details on this case?" she finally asked.

"From what I remember, there was a college student from LaCrosse doing research in Samuel's Cave. When he didn't return on schedule, his friends went searching for him. They found him just outside the mouth of the cave with an arrow through his heart. The fletching on the arrows matched those of the Oneota tribe but they weren't modern. They found this kid, Ronald Slick Beaver, and charged him with the murder."

"Why this kid?"

"His grandfather is, or I should say was, a historian about all the tribes in the Wisconsin area. He ran a small museum of ancient artifacts. The arrow that killed the victim matched some of the arrows in the grandfather's collection. It was only natural to suspect the grandson. He worked very closely with his grandfather and, if he wasn't in prison for the murder, he'd be the curator of that museum."

"Are you telling me you think Ronald was wrongfully convicted?"

"My friend thinks so, especially in light of the findings in your case. This kid has been in prison for the past six years, if it's been because of a mistake, we'd be doing him a great favor by clearing his name. Tomorrow is a teachers' day off so I don't have to work. I'd be happy to go to Waupun and talk to him. I don't mean to step on your toes, but if I could be of help, I'm more than willing to do anything I can. Besides, Judy has been bugging me to take her to the Oshkosh Outlet Mall. You know how much I hate shopping. I could leave her off there for the day and do a little research for you."

"I can't say no to you, but I'll have to run it past my boss. I'll call him and get right back to you."

They talked on about Rhonda's new job as well as how Phil was doing in his new position in Madison.

As soon as they hung up, Rhonda placed a call to Karl.

"I have some information I think might help our case," Rhonda said as soon as Karl said hello.

Rhonda outlined the case Phil told herself about in Wisconsin. "It sounds like this murder matches the ones we've been investigating."

"It certainly does. You said this former partner of yours is willing to go to the prison in Wisconsin to talk with the man convicted of it?"

"He is. He thinks Ronald Slick Beaver was wrongly convicted. In light of the information we've been uncovering here, I tend to agree with him."

"I can't stop him from going to the prison and interviewing the man. If it helps our case, I say tell him to go for it. Hopefully, we'll have some new information to go on by tomorrow night at this time."

After calling Phil back, Rhonda went into the kitchen to find Mark cleaning up. "I'm sorry I wrecked our romantic evening with calls about work."

"Honey, you know we can pick up where we left off. I've always known about your commitment to your job. It's one of the reasons I love you so much. Now, that wonderful whirlpool tub for two in the master bathroom is filled and ready for us to soak away the cares of the day."

Chapter Fifteen

As promised, the file from Wisconsin had been received via fax by the time Rhonda arrived at work the next morning. It sat on top of her desk along with several of the files from both of Roger Jenkins' shops.

"Karl told me you found another victim," Jenny said as she sat across from Rhonda to work on the files.

"Actually, it was my former partner. He happened to remember a case in Wisconsin that mirrors ours perfectly. The problem is they've already convicted someone for it."

"That could get nasty. So, tell me what we're looking for."

"The murder in Wisconsin was six years ago, so I'd like to start with that one. I think it's the most urgent, especially since there's a young man in prison who possibly could be free."

Rhonda looked over the file from Wisconsin that came complete with pictures of the murder weapon. There were also pictures taken from the museum depicting the ancient artifacts. They looked so much like the weapon used in the murder it was no wonder Ronald had been arrested. He certainly had accessibility to the arrows, but the grandfather swore none of his collection was missing.

"I think I might be onto something," Jenny declared.

Rhonda took the file her partner had been working on. The label read CUSTOM ORDERS and it was one of the files found at the Mesquite shop. After she rummaged through the contents of the file, Rhonda held up a picture matching the one on display at the Indian artifact museum in Wisconsin. Along with that one were pictures of war clubs, lances, knives, and many of the other murder weapons used by the man they were now referring to as the petroglyph killer.

"Well, this cinches it," Rhonda said. "We now know where our killer came by his weapons. This is beginning to feel like one of those puzzles where it's hard to find where the pieces go. If Roger was a middleman for these things, where did he get them?"

"I think we know that, considering the workroom we found in Mesquite. A better question might be is where did he get the peyote?"

Both women turned to see Karl standing in the doorway.

"Peyote?" they both said in unison.

"That's right. The lab has been working on those herbs you brought back from the shop. There was a lot of sage and other herbs to make tea, but we need to go back and search the rest of the shop. Somewhere in there he must have a bigger stash of the peyote than the small amount you brought back in one of those packets. Something tells me we know where all the money in the safety deposit boxes came from."

"Do you think we were ingesting that stuff?" Jenny asked, her voice sounding with horror.

Karl and Rhonda both laughed at the expression on her face.

"You've got to be kidding," Rhonda finally managed to say. "If the stuff the lab found is pure, I'm sure he sold it for an arm and a leg. It wouldn't surprise me to find out he was selling it to the college kids in the group, Society of the Arrow. I can only begin to imagine the high those kids could get off this stuff. It's even possible Roger had them thinking it was better for them than pot or any of the other drugs floating around campus."

"In other words, he was the Native American version of a dealer."

Rhonda's cell phone interrupted their conversation. Glancing at the display, Rhonda knew it was Phil calling to tell her about his meeting with Ronald Slick Beaver.

"What did you find?" Rhonda asked as soon as she answered.

"Ronald is an angry young man, and with good reason. Being a minority in a state prison is hard enough, but being one who is trying to tell everyone of his innocence it's even harder. I think you should come out here and talk to this guy for yourself. When I asked him how he thought someone got ahold of one of the arrows his grandfather kept in the museum, he said, it would be next to impossible. He also told me his grandfather never allowed pictures taken by the tourists."

Rhonda remembered the picture in the CUSTOM ORDER file and pulled it out. "I have a picture of the museum that matches the one your friend faxed over, that I found in a shop here in Nevada. Any idea how it could have gotten there?"

"Maybe someone asked the old man to send it out there, but I doubt it. With all the cell phones with cameras in them it would be easy to take pictures without being detected. Do you think your picture has anything to do with the murder here?"

"I most certainly do. I think what we found at the artifacts shop is just the tip of the iceberg."

"So, will you be coming back to Wisconsin to talk to this guy? Judy and I would love to have you come for a visit."

Rhonda looked at Karl. Since she'd put the phone on speaker, he'd heard the entire conversation.

"I've been thinking about the same thing," Karl said, making his presence known to Phil for the first time. "If I can get Rhonda and Jenny booked on the red eye tonight, can you get them into the prison to talk to Slick Beaver?"

"It shouldn't be a problem. Once you have the reservations made, Rhonda can give me a call. We've got enough room for both of them, and it will be great working with my old partner again. I can also arrange for my friend who worked the first case to meet with us. He's been doing some more digging ever since I talked to him about this last night. He wants to help and maybe free Ronald."

The thought of going back to Wisconsin intrigued Rhonda but not as much as possibly freeing an innocent man.

~ * ~

Mark drove Rhonda and Jenny to the airport for the red eye flight to Milwaukee. Even though Phil wanted to pick them up, Rhonda insisted on renting a vehicle so they wouldn't put Phil and Judy out. Besides, she liked to be independent and relying on someone to take her wherever she wanted to go wasn't her idea of how she liked to do things.

By seven in the morning, they arrived at Phil and Judy's house. Although they were both tired, Jenny was as eager to meet with Ronald Slick Beaver as Rhonda.

While Judy prepared breakfast for them, Rhonda and Jenny changed from comfortable traveling clothes to more professional suits.

"It's so good to have you here," Judy said, once Rhonda returned to the kitchen. "I know Phil misses having you around."

"I miss everyone here, but I'm making some good friends in Las Vegas."

"Did I hear my name mentioned," Jenny teased as she joined them.

"Not really, but you have to admit, we've hit it off since we first met on Sunday."

"What took you so long to get back into law enforcement?" Phil asked. "I thought that glowing recommendation I sent out there would have had those guys knocking down your door as soon as you arrived."

"You and a lot of other people. It all takes time; you have to know that. Besides, when I got there, I learned there was a hiring freeze at Metro. I was lucky to find a position with Clark County. It's a big force and there are a lot of opportunities."

"So, fill me in on this case you're working on," Phil pressed.

Rhonda related the information about finding the body in Red Rock Canyon as well as the cold case. She also told him about the cases they'd uncovered across the country that now included the one in Wisconsin six years earlier. She ended her narrative with the murder of Roger Jenkins in the Valley of Fire. She was careful to leave out the information about the drugs found at Roger's shop as well as the money and jewelry they now knew was worth millions of dollars. The cash had been counted and totaled two million, six hundred and seventy-five thousand, seven hundred and fifty dollars. They'd also had the jewelry appraised and the initial appraisal came in at least three million dollars.

Phil let out a low whistle. "You landed a nasty one this time. Does it remind you of anything?"

"I can't help but think about the Adkin's case, and of course, the one at your class reunion this past summer. The difference is this has been going on for the past eight years, if not more. So far we can pin at least twenty bodies on him."

"It could be a woman, though," Phil suggested.

"I seriously doubt that," Jenny commented. "From what we can ascertain, all this leads back to a college organization called the Society of the Arrow. It was more or less a chauvinist group, holding to the belief of many Native American tribes that women were to be protected, not to handle weapons. In each of the murders an ancient weapon has been used. Of course, you know that, because of the arrow that killed the college student here in Wisconsin."

Rhonda smiled. Her partner handled herself well. She knew Phil wanted all the information he could get about their case. Fortunately, both of them gave him only the facts that were already public knowledge.

~ * ~

Rhonda settled into the front seat of Phil's van, relieved to have him fighting the traffic not only on the city streets, Beltline, and Interstate but also through the country following HWY 51 to Waupun. From the back seat, Jenny marveled at the farmers harvesting corn and the beautiful colors of the autumn leaves that were just hitting their peak. Rhonda knew everything here was different from what Jenny was used to seeing in Nevada.

"This land is so flat," Jenny observed. "I kind of miss the mountains and all the red rock around Las Vegas."

Rhonda laughed at the comment. "Now you see why I miss Wisconsin so much."

By the time they pulled off onto HWY 26, Rhonda could feel her stomach begin to churn. She'd visited prisoners in the county jail, but this would be the first time she'd visited the state prison. "What can we expect when we meet Slick Beaver?"

"An angry young man. You'd be angry too if you'd been incarcerated for the past five years and were innocent."

"They're all innocent, aren't they?" Jenny asked.

"Of course they are, but once you meet this guy, you'll believe he's innocent too."

After going through all the security checkpoints, showing their identification about a dozen times, and surrendering not only their weapons, as well as any other metal they had with them, they were led into a visitor's room.

Rhonda envisioned talking to Ronald through thick glass over a phone but was pleasantly surprised when they were taken to a private room looking much like the interrogation rooms at the various departments where she'd worked. It took only a matter of minutes for the door on the opposite side of the room to open and Ronald entered, accompanied by two guards. She couldn't help noticing the heavy shackles on Ronald's wrists and ankles.

If it hadn't been for the shackles and the prison uniform, Rhonda would have thought she'd stepped onto one of the Northern Wisconsin reservations and was talking to any of the young men who grew up there. Ronald's jet-black hair hung in neat braids down to the middle of his back. His bronze skin color denoted the fact there had been no white ancestors in his family tree.

"Good morning," Rhonda greeted him, getting to her feet and extending her hand.

Even with his shackles, Ronald allowed her to shake his hand in greeting. "I'm surprised you'd come to visit me, Detective."

"You know who I am then?"

"When Officer Mason was here the other day, he said he was going to ask you to come. Do you think you can get me out of this mess?"

"I hope so. We agree with Officer Mason that you were a logical choice in this case because of your accessibility to weapons like the one used in the homicide. Add that to the fact you belonged to a group on campus that protested the geology department."

"I admit to being in that protest, but it wasn't against the geology department, it was against the people who defaced the petroglyphs with graffiti. These are ancient sites that deserve to be revered and maintained, not destroyed. I also had an alibi for the time and day of the incident and contrary to popular opinion just because we went to the same school we didn't know each other. I didn't hate him because he was white. I don't know if he hated me because I'm Native American. I've lived with the distrust of my people all my life."

"When you weren't in school, did you help out your grandfather in the museum?" Jenny asked.

"Of course, I did. It was a family business. I loved that place and planned to work there educating people about those who came before us for the rest of my life."

"Have you ever seen this man?" she pressed, taking a picture of Roger

Jenkins from her briefcase.

"Sure, that's Mr. Jenkins. He came in the off season to attend Grandfather's lectures. He was a good student. I remember him coming several times when I was in high school. Does he have something to do with all of this?"

"We're looking into it," Rhonda replied. "We think he was the middleman who supplied the weapons to whoever it is who is doing these killings."

"Killings?" Ronald questioned. "As in more than one?"

"I'm afraid so. There have been two in the Las Vegas area in the last five days as well as a cold case from eight years ago. We've also discovered several murders at archaeological sites around the country, including the one here."

"Do you think you could free me?"

"We hope so. I understand your grandfather passed away and I extend my deepest sympathy at your loss. I want to see you able to return to the museum and continue the work he started. I checked it out on the internet and the next time I'm back in Wisconsin, I'd enjoy having you give me a tour and hear one of your lectures."

For the first time, Ronald's features softened, and a hint of a smile graced his lips. "Thank you, Detective. I'll be pleased to show you everything in our collection."

~ * ~

"Would you like to see the site where the murder took place six years ago?" Phil asked as they pulled back onto the highway.

"You know we would," Rhonda replied. "Are you going to take us there or just tease us? If I remember, it's quite a drive from here."

"From here, yes, it is, but I promised Judy I'd take her up to see the petroglyphs this weekend. When do you have to fly back to Vegas?"

Before Rhonda could answer, her cell phone rang. "Pohs here," she answered automatically.

"Rhonda, it's Karl. Did you get to the prison yet?"

"We're just leaving. Phil mentioned going to the murder site tomorrow."

"I'm afraid you're going to have to take a rain check on your field trip. We've had some new developments out here. I've made reservations for you on the flight tonight out of Milwaukee."

"What kind of developments?"

"It's nothing I want to go into over the phone. I checked your flight, and it gets in around eleven tonight. I'll meet you at the airport and save your husband a trip into Las Vegas. That way I can brief you on the way back to your place."

"That doesn't sound good," Jenny commented.

"It's not. As soon as we get back to your place, we have to get ready to go back to Milwaukee and catch a late flight to Vegas. Karl wouldn't say what was going on, but he did say there had been some new developments in the case."

"Judy's going to be disappointed about you going back so soon, but she knows what it means to be in law enforcement. She should, she's been married to me long enough not to plan on anything."

"Are you still planning to go to the petroglyphs tomorrow?" Jenny asked.

"I can't use the excuse that duty calls," Phil said with a wink. "Judy and I are both looking forward to seeing them. With the kids grown and out of the house, we can do things like this, especially with my new job. Why do you ask?"

"I would appreciate it if you'd send us pictures. I want to know what Ronald meant by the graffiti on the rocks."

"I'm sorry we aren't going to get to meet your friend though. I think there's a lot he can tell us about this case. Maybe you can have him call me next week."

"You know I can," Phil agreed. "He'll be disappointed about not getting to meet you, but it can't be helped."

Chapter Sixteen

Karl waited for them in the baggage check area. As much as Rhonda wished Mark would be the one meeting them, she knew Karl called and told him he'd be meeting their flight and bringing them home. Mark confirmed Karl's call when they talked just before the plane took off from Milwaukee.

The back-to-back flight to and from Wisconsin drained Rhonda. The last thing she wanted was to discuss the case with Karl as he drove them to Searchlight.

"I know the timing is bad. I should have let you stay in Wisconsin a little longer, but this was too important not to have you in on it. Someone set fire to Jenkins' shop in Las Vegas early this morning. Thank goodness this is the town that never sleeps. A homeless guy called it in before there was damage to much more than the front area. At least you got out all the important stuff the other day."

"Did you get a description of the arsonist?" Jenny asked.

"Not really. The guy who called it in was drunk as a skunk, but he did say it was an Indian. That seems to be the consensus in this case. Unfortunately, I have my doubts about any of the Native American population being involved. Whoever is behind this is what I've always called a wannabe Indian."

"Did IT get anything off the computers?"

"I talked to them before I left work today and they said there's a ton of information for them to sift through. I doubt we'll know anything before Monday morning. I think you can enjoy the next couple of days off before we start in on this again."

By the time Karl left Rhonda off at the house, she was fuming. As much as she tried to stay calm when Mark met her at the door, she exploded.

"I can't believe Karl dragged us back here tonight."

"Don't blame him for that. From the way things sounded when he called me about picking you up at the airport, I think he's getting pressure from on high. As for that fire, it's been on the news all day. I drove past the shop on my way home from work today. The front of the shop looks like a total loss. Thank goodness the fire department got there when they did. The way the media is making it sound, the back of the shop is still intact and that's where the most valuable artifacts are."

Rhonda took a cleansing breath. It had been a long two days and, other than the sandwiches Judy fixed for them before they left for the airport, she'd eaten nothing since breakfast.

"I know you're tired," Mark said, breaking into her thoughts, "but I think you need to eat something. I've got a light supper made for you and then I plan to get you off to bed."

"You're right of course. I am hungry and tired. The media is right, too. From what I could tell, some of the stuff in the back of Roger's shop is invaluable. I know there are a lot of replicas there, but from what I could see there are also some ancient artifacts. We took as much as we could the other day, but there is so much more there. From what Karl said, on the trip back from the airport, they started taking the remainder of the inventory into protective custody until the State Historical Society can sort through everything and see what is authentic and what is mere junk."

Mark took her in his arms and kissed her long and hard. "For now, it's just you and me. We're going to have supper and then go to bed. If we can believe Karl, we can sleep in tomorrow and Sunday. I plan to take you to Hoover Dam and play tourist for the day on Sunday, complete with a romantic dinner at the top of the Stratosphere. As you might recall, that was the plan for last week before all hell broke loose out at Red Rock Canyon. I owe you an anniversary dinner, complete with champagne and all the romance I can produce for you."

Rhonda melted into Mark's arms. No matter what was going on with her job, he was her rock, the one constant in her life. For this weekend, she was determined to forget about the high-profile case she and Jenny were working on and enjoy everything Mark planned for her.

~ * ~

Rhonda couldn't believe how late she slept on Saturday morning.

Although Mark kept busy with things around the house, he insisted she relax with a good book. His excuse was they were going to have a busy day on Sunday and after the trip to Wisconsin, Rhonda needed her rest.

Hoover Dam was everything the tourist guides promised. Rhonda was awed by the massive structure connecting Nevada and Arizona. It was, indeed, an amazing marvel of modern technology.

Later, from the top of the Stratosphere, Rhonda and Mark watched as evening fell and the city below them came to life in lights of every imaginable color, promising the tourists who flocked here whatever pleasures they craved.

"To us," Mark said, holding up a glass of champagne. "I never expected when we got married our lives would take so many different twists and turns."

"Me either," Rhonda agreed. "At that time, we'd both graduated from college and I was in the police academy at the technical college. I thought I'd always be a beat cop and here I am a homicide detective with Clark County. It's a long way away from small town Wisconsin where I first started my career."

"You know I worried about you when I first took the job out here, but I think you're like a cat. You certainly landed on your feet. I know this is a difficult case, but I have all the confidence in the world in you."

Chapter Seventeen

Monday morning, Rhonda reluctantly pulled herself out of bed and got ready to go to work. After two days of rest and relaxation, she once again had to think about the baffling case she had been working on for over a week. For some reason it seemed more like months than just eight days.

"We've had someone monitoring the Society of the Arrow website ever since we first found out about them," Karl advised them when they arrived at the office. "There was a post on Sunday that the IT department is tracking down."

Rhonda looked at the printout. The message was clearly an admission of guilt. *RIP Racing Horse. Sorry you had to be sacrificed, but it was for the good of the organization. You knew too many of our secrets, including the fact we are alive, well and still prospering. It's too bad the fire didn't destroy all of our secrets. – THE SOCIETY OF THE ARROW*

She took a deep breath as she reread the posting. "Do you think we can figure out who posted this?"

"Like I said before, the IT department is working on it. They tell me they can find out who posted this and where they were at the time. The University has given permission to look into it. It will just take time is all."

Rhonda mentally went over all the players in this drama. She immediately dismissed Lloyd Charging Antelope Carpenter. His reaction to the thought the murders were connected to the Society of the Arrow was one of shock. Steven Flying Arrow Andrews hadn't responded to any of her requests for an interview, so she had no reason to count him out. It was George Spanton who intrigued her the most. She'd been unable to find the name of his alter ego, but his reaction to her visit to his office caused her to be suspicious.

Her musings were interrupted by a call. She was surprised to find Alex Meyers on the other end of the line. "I think you left me a message last week. I've been working on a tough case and this was the first chance I had to get back to you."

"Thank you. I was wondering what you remembered about a case you worked eight years ago when you were with Clark County?"

"If you mean that fiasco in Keyhole Canyon, I'd really like to forget it, but it haunts me. That case was the reason I left Clark County."

"What do you mean?" Rhonda asked, before putting her phone on speaker mode.

"I always thought I was lucky to be partnered with Jack Spanton. Boy was I wrong. From the minute we caught that case he started acting strange. We talked to a couple of hikers and as soon as they mentioned that damned Society of the Arrow, he dismissed everything they had to say. I always suspected those kids had something to do with that murder, but Jack wouldn't hear any of it. I wanted to report it, but he was not only the senior member of the force, but he was also the primary on the case. I tried going over his head, but no one would listen to me. After that I started looking for a new position. Luckily, my wife had a chance to take a job in Orange County, so my taking the job in Los Angeles only made sense."

"What can you tell me about the Society of the Arrow?"

"I did a lot of research on them at the time. Originally, they were a great group, but at the time of the murder they had gotten into drugs quite heavily. Granted they were natural drugs, but then marijuana is a natural plant too. It doesn't mean it was any less dangerous. I had a lot of contact with a guy called Roger Racing Horse Jenkins, but I realized he was little more than a computer geek and had a real interest in the Native American Culture. If I were looking into this case again, I'd check out George Spanton and a guy by the name of Soaring Eagle. I don't remember his real name, but it shouldn't be too hard to find. He was one of the people connected with the Society of the Arrow. What I want to know is why you're interested in this case eight years after the fact?"

Rhonda related the facts regarding the other cases that seemed to be related to the incident in Keyhole Canyon, including the murder of Roger Jenkins and the arson to his shop.

"Well, I wish you luck. I've got notes on this case at my home. If I come up with anything, I'll get back to you. I'll be anxious to know what you find out. I do have a vested interest in this whole thing, you know."

Rhonda agreed. Unfortunately, the phone call from Alex brought up more questions than it did answers. As soon as she hung up, Rhonda started looking for any listing for the name of Soaring Eagle among the lists of students involved with the Society of the Arrow.

"I don't see a thing about Soaring Eagle in any of these lists," Rhonda complained.

"I think I found it," Jenny said, turning her computer screen in Rhonda's direction. "I found an old list with the name Robert Soaring Eagle Burton on it. From what this says, he was asked to leave the group for inappropriate behavior."

"Did you say Robert Burton?" Karl asked.

"Why? Is that a name we should be familiar with?"

"Not you, but I know the name. He's the son of a former casino owner and a showgirl. They both died in a car accident and neither family wanted anything to do with their son. He was highly intelligent and got into the University. In his senior year he got into some trouble and was expelled from the University. It was quite a scandal at the time."

"What kind of trouble would get a student expelled?"

"If I remember correctly, Bob and a friend hacked into the University's computer and got the final exams for several of the classes, then sold them to the students. At the time Bob wouldn't name his accomplice, but now it all makes sense. Something tells me his partner in crime was Roger Jenkins."

"So why kill Jenkins?" Jenny asked.

"That's what they pay us the big bucks to figure out," Karl teased. "The last I heard of Burton, he was running some internet company and traveling around the country promoting it. To be truthful, he's been giving Las Vegas and Roger a wide berth for the past eight years. It could be he wanted to distance himself from this area. It could be after the murder at Red Rock he and Roger had a falling out. If Roger has been his supplier over the years, I can understand him wanting Bob to stay away from Vegas."

"That ties it up in a neat package, but how do we go about finding the connection?" Rhonda inquired. As soon as she said the words, she realized the answer to her question was somewhere within Roger's shop. If all that was burned was the front where the fake artifacts were displayed, there had to be things in the back of the shop they could use to lead them to Bob Burton and, however, many of the members of the Society of the Arrow were still active.

Chapter Eighteen

While the IT department scoured Roger's computers for information, Rhonda and Jenny made another trip down to the now burned-out shop. Even though they'd been told most of the artifacts from the back of the shop had been taken into protective custody, Rhonda wanted to be sure nothing was missed.

"Just what are we looking for?" Jenny asked.

"I'm not sure, but there's got to be something here we've overlooked."

After an hour of going through the charred rubble in the front of the shop as well as the empty rooms in the back, Rhonda almost tripped over something the CSI people overlooked when they cleaned out the shop.

"I think this might be something," she said holding up a fireproof safe. "The only problem I see is how to get into it."

Jenny laughed. "You must not watch much TV."

She held the box out in front of her before dropping it on the floor. Once it hit the hard surface the lip popped open spilling the contents across the dusty boards.

"Where did you learn something like that?"

"My boyfriend likes that show Storage Wars. I saw them do it on one of the episodes I managed to watch."

Rhonda dropped to her knees and started shuffling through the contents of the box. "I knew we were missing something," Rhonda said, as she held up a manila envelope.

Taking out the contents, she was surprised to find a key to yet another safe deposit box as well as a bank book for an account she was sure no one ever knew about. The name on the bank account was Society of the Arrow.

"Why would a defunct organization need a bank account with over three hundred thousand dollars in it?"

Jenny reached over and took the bank book out of Rhonda's hands. On a piece of paper, they found in the envelope they saw the people authorized to use the account were Robert Burton and Roger Jenkins.

~ * ~

Back at the office, Rhonda and Jenny were overwhelmed by the amount of paperwork from the IT department with the information taken from Roger's many computers.

"Where do you think we should start?" Jenny asked.

Rhonda took a deep breath before picking up the folder marked CUSTOM ORDER. "We found the information linking Jenkins to the murder in Wisconsin in this file. Something tells me we'll find links to the other murders here. I say we start by listing the murders from out of state by date and listing the murder weapons and see if we can find corresponding orders sent to the shop. If Roger was working with Burton, or Soaring Eagle, it only makes sense he would have been filling the orders to the specifications he wanted."

"Another thing I'd like to check is to see if we can get a picture of Burton, possibly one six years old," Jenny suggested. "Ronald said there was a man in the museum who was very interested in the arrows like the one used in the murder at the petroglyphs. Once we find one, we can get a copy sent to your friend Phil, he could show it to Ronald. If we're right about this lead, it's possible Ronald might be able to identify him."

"I want to see Detective Pohs." Rhonda heard a man at the front desk say.

"May I ask your name?"

"I'm Steven Flying Arrow Anders. She left a message on my phone. I got the message when I returned home from vacation last night."

Rhonda got up from her desk and went out to greet the man who'd come to see her. "I'm Detective Pohs," she said, extending her hand. "I thought I'd hear back from you last week."

"I've been out of the country on a cruise with my wife. When we heard the message and then got caught up on the news, my wife thought I should come down here in person to talk to you. I'm assuming this has something to do with that business in Red Rock Canyon."

"That's right. Would you like to come back to my office so we can talk in private about this?"

Steven agreed and followed Rhonda not back to her cubicle, but to Karl's office.

"I have several questions I'd like to ask you," Rhonda said once they were in the office. "Do you mind if I tape our conversation?"

"Is that standard procedure?"

"It's something I like to do then there's no question about what was said by either of us."

"If that's the case, I have no problem with it."

"Thank you. It's for your protection as well as for mine. Do you know anything about the murder?"

"Not really. My wife and I have been out of the country for the last two weeks. I also had a message from Lloyd Carpenter. I think you know him as Charging Antelope. He also left a message on my machine saying you were at his office asking about the Society of the Arrow. I figured that's where you got my name. We were both members of the group before they disbanded. That was a while ago."

"Do you know why they disbanded?"

"I got out when I realized they were more interested in drugs than they were in the study of the ancient Native American culture. Back twenty years ago, when more people were into the drugs, I don't think it was much of a problem, but I just couldn't become involved."

"Why couldn't you be involved?" Rhonda pressed.

"I was completing my master's degree when I was involved with that group. When I told them I didn't want any part of the drugs I was politely told not to come back to any of their meetings. It was just as well, since after graduation, I got a position as a curator at a museum in Reno, dealing in Native American artifacts."

The mention of the museum Steven worked at piqued Rhonda's interest. "What do you know about Roger Jenkins?"

"He was the webmaster for the Society of the Arrow when I was in school. I also dealt with him for artifacts for the museum. He has one of the best collections in the area. He also knows how to get some wonderful recreations. I've used some of his things for displays when I couldn't get the authentic items."

"Do you also know Robert Soaring Eagle Burton?"

Steven wrinkled his brow as though contemplating the name. "I can't say as I do. Is he someone I should know?"

"I think you're lucky you don't know him. Have you heard about Mr. Jenkins' death?"

"Roger is dead? How? When?"

Rhonda related the details of Roger's murder and the subsequent fire at his shop to Steven.

"It makes sense," Steven said. "Mouse was a notorious renegade who stole from the whites. Of course, he only stole food to feed his people, but the whites wanted him dead. Mouse's Tank is where he was finally captured. I always wondered where Roger got some of his artifacts. Do you think this was retaliation for him stealing what belonged to the ancients of this area?"

"I don't think so, but I do think he could be linked to a string of murders all taking place at sites of rock paintings and petroglyphs."

Steven's face went white. "Do you think it was linked to that murder at Keyhole Canyon years ago?"

"That one and almost twenty more. Do you know anything about the first one?"

"Just the rumors that went around the University whenever anyone mentioned the Society of the Arrow."

"What rumors?"

"It was said someone in the organization was behind the murder at Keyhole, but it was never proved because one of the members' dads was a cop and they got a free pass. Of course, I didn't hear any of that until after I was asked to leave the group. I found out no one dared to mention it to any of the members. As soon as I was no longer one of them, I heard all the dirty little secrets."

"Why didn't you come forward with this information before?"

Steven licked his lips, obviously nervous about his answer. "At the time I didn't have any hard facts. I was certain no one would believe me, especially since there was a cop's kid involved."

Rhonda had to admit she did believe what Steven told her. Of course, it corresponded with the story they'd heard from the Parker brothers about the involvement of George Spanton's father.

"Would you excuse me for a minute?" Rhonda asked as she got up to leave Karl's office.

"Did you hear what Anders had to say?" she asked when she met Karl and Jenny in the hall.

"I didn't get all of it, but I'm hoping you were taping it."

"I always tape my interviews and I did get permission from Mr. Anders before I started. From what he said, I'm sure he had nothing to do with this, but he did tell us more than anyone has so far. I think we need to pay another visit to George Spanton and maybe invite him to come to our house for a visit."

Karl agreed and said he would contact George and ask him to come in for an official interview. While Karl went to make the arrangements to have George brought in for questioning, Rhonda returned to the office where she'd been interviewing Steven.

"I just have one more question for you," she said once she entered the room. "Do you know George Spanton?"

Steven nodded sagely. "His name in the organization was Red Hawk. From what I heard around school, he was the cop's kid that squelched the investigation of the murder at Keyhole Canyon. I always wondered if he was involved, but like I said before, I didn't have any solid evidence to go on. He was the one who told me I was no longer welcome in the group."

Rhonda could feel a knot starting to form in her stomach. With all her heart she didn't want to find out a cop was privy to information that could have solved the case and hadn't followed up on it.

Rhonda got to her feet and extended her hand to Steven. "Thank you for coming in. Your information has been very helpful. If I have any further questions, I'll be in touch with you."

"If I think of anything more, I'll let you know. I can't believe there are so many murders associated with the Society of the Arrow. I wish I'd said something years ago, but I didn't know if anyone would believe me, especially when Officer Spanton wasn't interested in hearing anything about the group being involved."

Chapter Nineteen

"I think the interview went quite well," Rhonda commented as she shared a cup of coffee with Jenny. "I certainly learned a lot about the Society of the Arrow that I didn't know before. I think the biggest revelation was about the number of drugs they were using."

"Do you think they were street drugs?"

"Probably, but I think a lot of it was peyote. From everything we've heard, these guys were hell bent on being the same as the Native Americans. All it took was one look at Roger and it wasn't hard to tell how immersed he was in the culture."

"While you were interviewing Steven, I got a report from the lab. Most of the dried herbs we got from the front of Roger's shop were sage and other local plants, but they did find a large stash of peyote, so I think you're right about that part of it. We've also gotten a warrant to open the safe deposit box we found the key for yesterday. It should be interesting to see what we find in it."

Jenny finished her coffee and went back to her own cubicle to prepare to go to the bank and open the safe deposit box. Before Rhonda could join her, Karl appeared at the door of her cubicle.

"I know you got permission to open that safe deposit box. Unfortunately, that will have to wait. I need to have you go down to Spanton's apartment. It seems he never arrived for work this morning. The people from the Palms have tried calling him but they can't get an answer either at his home or on his cell."

With what she'd just learned from Steven Anders, Rhonda worried about what they would find when they arrived at the apartment. Putting down her coffee cup, she hurried out to the car to meet Jenny.

"Are you ready to go to the bank?" Jenny asked.

"Change of plans. Karl got word George Spanton didn't show up for work this morning and isn't answering his phone. We're going over to his apartment. Here's the address Karl gave me. Hopefully we can get in."

Outside the apartment building, they were met by two uniformed officers from Clark County as well as two from Metro. "You must be Detective Pohs," the Clark County deputy greeted her. "It's good to see you, too, Jenny."

"It's good to see you too, Kev. Rhonda Pohs, this is my boyfriend, Kevin Richardson."

Rhonda shook hands with the young man. "Do I have to ask what you're doing here?" she asked.

"We got a call to pick up a warrant to get into Spanton's apartment. Since this is a secure building, you can't just walk up to his apartment door."

Rhonda smiled. She'd been to buildings like this one before and knew getting past the doorman would require a warrant. As though she'd been given a magic key, the warrant worked wonders. In no time they were on the eighteenth floor heading toward the apartment number the doorman gave them.

To her surprise the door stood ajar as though George was expecting company. "Mr. Spanton, this is Detective Pohs. I'm coming in."

Behind her she heard the deputies pull their guns.

"If you're here, please call out."

She only had to walk through the kitchen before she saw George Spanton sprawled across the white leather couch that was now stained with blood. Kevin went over to the couch to check for a pulse.

"He's dead. This looks like suicide. He slit his wrists. I'll call for the coroner but I'm willing to bet he's been dead since sometime last night."

Rhonda agreed. As she looked around the apartment, she saw a spiral notebook on the coffee table. After putting on a pair of gloves, she picked up the notebook and saw there were several handwritten pages.

"I think I just found the suicide note," she said as she quickly scanned the blood-spattered page.

"What does it say?" Jenny asked.

Rhonda looked at the beginning of the note and tried to decipher the scrawl she could only assume belonged to George.

"My name is George Spanton. Things are getting too weird for me. Back when we killed that kid in Keyhole Canyon, we were all high as kites and didn't take kindly to some queer invading our group. I was able to get my old man to lay off the group, but what has happened these past few days is something I can no longer condone.

"I thought that one killing was going to be the only one but now there's been another killing in Red Rock Canyon and Roger is dead. I'd rather take my own life than become the next one to be sacrificed. Yes, I said sacrificed. After the Red Rock Canyon thing we're all at risk.

"Roger was just the first. With all the flack this is getting, I know Red Hawk will want all of us dead. I'm guilty of murder just as he is, but I don't want to die at his hands or go to prison. I've already warned Lloyd but don't know how to get ahold of the others. It's best if I end things now rather than suffer Red Hawk's wrath or live like a caged animal."

Rhonda looked up at Jenny, totally shaken by what she'd just read. "We've got to talk to Lloyd Carpenter again. I have a feeling he knows more than he's saying. If George thought he was in danger, he had to be in Keyhole Canyon when the murder took place. I wish I knew who the rest of them were. It looks to me like anyone who was in the Society of the Arrow could be a potential victim."

Rhonda was aware someone called for the coroner when not only the coroner but also CSI, EMT's and the fire department crowded into the apartment. Once they realized the man was already dead, everyone but the coroner and CSI left to attend to other emergencies.

Rhonda slipped the suicide note into an evidence bag and looked around the apartment for any other evidence. Once the body was moved, she found the knife George used on his wrists and put that into another bag to preserve any fingerprints that might still be on the handle. If this was indeed a suicide there would only be one set of prints on the knife, where if it had been murder there would be others.

"Why do you think the door was open?" Jenny asked, breaking into Rhonda's internal musings.

"It's possible, being a cop's kid, he wanted his body to be found. He knew if he left his door ajar, someone might be curious enough to come in to investigate. He might have thought they would have come in time to save his life, but the way this note reads, he was set on taking his own life."

Their conversation took Rhonda's mind from the coroner positioning the body into the body bag and getting it onto the gurney to take it to the morgue.

"Do you know if he has anyone who can come down and identify the body?"

Rhonda and Jenny exchanged anxious glances. "We'll check through the papers here at the apartment and see if we can find someone. We do know his father is dead but have no information on his mother or siblings."

With the body gone, Rhonda went through the desk sitting across from the couch and next to the big screen TV to see if she could find anything that would indicate an address for any family members. After going through two drawers, she finally located an address book. She quickly turned to the page with the letter 'S' listed, she found three names she felt were worth looking into. Mary Grace Spanton lived in Henderson, Jocelyn Spanton lived in Los Angeles and Katie Elizabeth Spanton was listed as being in Albuquerque, New Mexico.

"I think we start with Mary Grace in Henderson. She's the closest and I have a feeling she might be George's mother."

Jenny agreed and they were getting ready to leave for Henderson to make a condolence call when Rhonda's phone rang.

"I know you're in the middle of this mess, but you need to get over to that bank with the warrant to open the safe deposit box. I just had a call from the bank manager, and they have a man there trying to access the Society of the Arrow account. Because of the amount of money in the account, they told him he'd have to wait for them to get the money from the main branch. I have a feeling this guy could be Robert Burton."

"We were just getting ready to go out to Henderson and make a condolence call on Mary Grace Spanton. It's possible she's George's mother."

"I'll take care of the notification and see if she can come in to give a positive identification of the body. I need the two of you to go over to the bank while they're still able to detain him."

Rhonda agreed, but she was torn. She wanted to meet with Mary Grace Spanton and yet she knew she needed to get to the bank and confront Robert Burton.

~ * ~

"My name is on that goddamned account. I showed you my ID and did everything but give you my left nut. What more do I have to do to get my money?"

Rhonda could hear Robert Burton ranting even before she entered the bank.

"I'm sorry, Mr. Burton, but it takes time to get three hundred thousand dollars in cash. I told you before, I've ordered it from our main branch, and it should be here any minute."

"It better be, you little bitch, or you'll be sorry. You have no idea who I am. I'm Dr. Robert Burton. I'm well respected in my field and I have a plane to catch in two hours. You're holding me up. If I miss that flight, you're screwed."

Rhonda took the opportunity to approach the man. "I'm Detective Rhonda Pohs, Dr. Burton, and I'd like you to come down to headquarters so we can ask you a few questions."

"I have nothing to say to you, bitch. What is it with this fucked up town anyway? Doesn't anyone hire men anymore?"

"I'm a man, Dr. Burton," Karl said from behind them. "I hired these young women, and it was because they're the best people for the job. I'm here to arrest you for the murders of Nancy Callahan and Roger Jenkins for starters. You have the right to remain silent…"

"Yeah, yeah, yeah, I know all that Miranda Rights crap. You don't know who you're dealing with here. I'm Dr. Robert Burton. I'm one of the foremost professors of Native American History in this country. You have no right to arrest me."

"We have every right to arrest you. Now come along peacefully. Once we're down at the station, you'll be able to tell us your side of things."

Rhonda watched as two uniformed officers entered the bank and escorted Burton from the premises to a waiting squad car.

"I thought you might like some help. I also picked up the warrant you need to open the safe deposit box."

They'd left the office in such a hurry to check on George Spanton, they hadn't waited for the necessary paperwork to gain entry into the safe deposit box in the name of the Society of the Arrow at this bank.

Once Karl showed the bank manager the warrant, they had no problem getting access to the sealed box. They were escorted to a small room and Karl unlocked the lid. Rhonda didn't realize she'd been holding her breath until the lid of the box opened and the contents were revealed. If she thought the box would be filled with cash and jewelry as were the other boxes Roger had in his name, she was mistaken. Rather than anything with monetary value the box was filled with several journals. On the cover of each was the title SECRETS OF THE SOCIETY OF THE ARROW.

By the time they drove to the office, Rhonda read enough to incriminate more than one of the members of the society. In every entry, the name Robert Red Hawk Burton was mentioned at least one time, Burton was orchestrating not only the murders in Nevada but also those around the country that until now were considered unsolved.

~ * ~

"Where the hell have you been?" Robert demanded when Rhonda entered the interrogation room.

"Just collecting a little more evidence against you," she replied.

For emphasis she placed one of the journals on the table between them.

"What the fuck is that?"

"You don't know? I've had a great time reading about the Society of the Arrow. It sounds like quite an organization. It seems that Roger Jenkins was more than just the webmaster for the organization. He was the historian as well."

"I have no idea what you're talking about."

"I'm sure you don't. I thought we could start by talking about the murder of Roger Jenkins in the Valley of Fire."

"I don't have to say jack shit to you, lady. I want to talk to my lawyer."

"Oh, I didn't know you'd called a lawyer. Of course, that's your prerogative. Have you already called him?"

"You know I haven't. I've been stuck in the goddamn room waiting for some bimbo detective to get here. I haven't even been given my one phone call."

"I'm sorry about that, Dr. Burton. I'll make sure you have a phone brought into you."

"I don't have no fuckin' lawyer in this suck ass town."

"If you can't afford a lawyer, I can make certain a public defender is brought here for you."

Burton's face turned red and Rhonda was sure she could see steam billowing from his ears.

"I can afford the most expensive lawyer in this town. I just don't know who the fuck they are. If you're going to bring me a fuckin' phone, you'd better bring me a listing of the lawyers in this town."

Rhonda nodded and got up to leave the room. Once outside she breathed a sigh of relief. "Do you know how hard it was for me not to jump across the table and throttle that bastard?"

Karl chuckled. "I understand you completely. I think I should be the one to bring in the phone and the listing. I'd hate to have to arrest you for murder before you've been on the force for a month."

Rhonda smiled at his comment. It was rare for her to completely lose control, but Robert Burton managed to push her buttons to the point of meltdown. She watched from the other side of the two-way mirror in the interrogation room as Karl came in with the phone and phone book.

"I didn't think the Bimbo could handle it. I can't believe you think she's the best person for the job. I'm pleased to think you have enough balls to come in here yourself."

"It's not that Detective Pohs can't handle this. I came in here to keep her from killing you. I've seen some bad ass characters come through this jail, but I've never seen any that can hold a candle to you."

Karl laid the paper with the listings of area lawyers on the table. "You want to call a lawyer; I'll be more than happy to leave you in here to see if you can find one who will take your case. While you do that, I'll be out reading through the journals Roger Jenkins left."

"That son of a bitch didn't keep no goddamn journals. I know how cops are. They want to be right so badly they manufacture evidence when they can't produce the real thing. If there were any journals, I would have…"

"You would have what, Dr. Burton? Are you telling me you were at the shop after Roger was killed?"

"I told the bitch I didn't have to say anything to her and that goes double for you. Just give me that goddamn phone and get the fuck out of here."

Chapter Twenty

Once Burton evoked his right to a lawyer, Rhonda went back to her cubical where she found Jenny going over the journals.

"This guy kept a detailed report of everything that went on within the group over the years. It starts when he first meets Dr. Burton during his freshman year at UNLV."

She handed the spiral notebook over to Rhonda.

I knew my choice to study Native American culture was the right one today when I met Dr. Robert Burton. Although he's a professor, he doesn't teach at any of the schools. Instead, he travels around the country enlightening students about the wonders of the ancient world and promoting his group Society of the Arrow.

Just listening to his lecture today ignited a spark within me. He must have noticed it because he singled me out to join his group. I will be attending my first meeting this weekend. He told me I'd be witnessing an ancient religious ceremony.

I went to the meeting on Saturday morning. We went out to a site in Grapevine Canyon where there are a lot of petroglyphs. Dr. Burton informed us he is a shaman and is able to go into a trancelike state. He left us to study the petroglyphs and when he returned, he was dressed in full regalia. He looked very much like the shaman I've seen in the movies.

I think he was smoking something funny in his pipe because he went into a trance and started talking in a strange language. I can only compare it to someone talking in tongues like in the Bible. He certainly put on quite a show. One of the older members took a puff on the pipe and told us it was nasty shit. I didn't have the balls to try it and neither did any of the other members.

About an hour later Dr. Burton came out of his trance and told us the ancients talked to him and told him from this day forward we were to call him Soaring Eagle. He said it was like going on a vision quest without going out alone in the wilderness for several days without food or water.

He also gave me my name from the ancients. He told me from here on in I would be called Racing Horse since that is the name the ancients chose for me. Later I asked how the ancients knew about horses since they weren't brought to this continent until they came with the Spanish Conquistadors. He told me the ancients know everything from the beginning of time to the end of days. I was thrilled to have such an honor bestowed on me.

Rhonda set aside the journal. "Do you think Burton was smoking peyote?"

"It's possible," Jenny replied. "It certainly would account for the trancelike state and the visions he had. I've been thumbing through several of these books and found the one from the time of Gerald Kaiser's murder. I think you'll find this passage quite interesting."

I was invited to a ceremony that was being held at Keyhole Canyon. It was a weekend retreat and Soaring Eagle promised me I would have a wonderful time. Since I've been the webmaster ever since 1996. Everyone was there with us, including Hunting Hawk, Wounded Beaver, and Fighting Bear.

There were also several underclassmen with us but most of them left after the first day. The only one who remained was Jerry Kaiser. He wanted to be a member of the group so badly. Soaring Eagle told him if he stayed for the second day, he would go through the ceremony to join the group. Of course, I knew different. It was common knowledge that Jerry was gay and Soaring Eagle couldn't abide anyone in the gay community.

I watched as Soaring Eagle sacrificed Jerry and the others saw it too. Thank goodness George's father believed him when he said the group had nothing to do with the murder and went on to check out other avenues. If he hadn't, we would have all been arrested and spent the rest of our lives on death row. I know we'll all burn in hell for what we did. Jerry's parents deserve to know the truth behind his death.

"Wow," Rhonda said almost in a half whisper. "This means that two of the people involved in the murder are already dead, a third is in custody but that leaves three of them unaccounted for. I think it's time we found out about Darrell Williams, Alan Knilans and Joseph Roberts. I'll see if we can get warrants for their arrests since there is no statute of limitations for murder."

"Before you do that, you'd better look at some of these other journals.

I've pulled the ones that correspond with the other murders around the country. This is the one for the time of the murder in Wisconsin."

I got an order today from Soaring Eagle. I wish I could pull out of this shit, but if I do, he could easily incriminate me for that business with Jerry Kaiser. I don't know why he can't use one of the arrows he's ordered in the past, but he says this one has to have a fletching like the one in the picture. Of course, I'll be able to make one, but why he needs it is beyond me. That man must have one of the most extensive collections of ancient weapons in the country. I wonder what he does with all of them.

"Does this mean Roger was the one making all the weapons used in the murders?" Rhonda asked.

"It sounds like it," Jenny agreed. "We didn't find anything that looked like a workshop at the store in Vegas. I wonder if he did his work in the one at Mesquite or if he had another location we haven't found yet. With so much going on, we certainly haven't had enough time to go through all the files we found at his place here before the fire."

Rhonda thought for a moment before answering. "It could be. I have a feeling we'll find out more about Soaring Eagle by reading the rest of these journals. Since we have the dates of the murders that took place across the country, we can see if there are corresponding entries."

Several hours later, Rhonda realized just how deeply not only Dr. Burton but also Roger were involved in the unsolved cases throughout the country. It didn't take long to see each of the ancient weapons used in the murders were fashioned by Roger even if he didn't know what they were being used for.

"You have to read this entry," Jenny declared as she held up the last journal in the pile.

Rhonda picked it up and read what she was looking at. The date denoted it was written the morning after Nancy Callahan's murder at Red Rock Canyon.

Soaring Eagle came into the shop this morning. He told me about the murder of the woman in Red Rock Canyon. I asked what he knew about it and he told me I had to be an idiot if I hadn't figured out I'd been the one supplying him with the weapons for the sacrifices.

I asked him why he killed that woman, and he told me it was because she was violating the ancients by taking pictures of them. He also said they were not for women to gaze upon, and he was enraged when he saw her.

I told him women were becoming more and more involved in archaeology and are more than likely more meticulous than the men.

He came back with how the ancients told him women who participated in things like this should be sacrificed. He said they were worse than the gays and we both knew how he felt about them.

I'm afraid I'm in this so deeply I can never get out. I know I made the knife that killed her. If I thought I was going to burn in hell for Jerry's murder I don't know what will happen to me because of this one.

She glanced down and saw the next entry was on the day they found the shop in Las Vegas closed for business.

Soaring Eagle called me today and told me to come out to the Valley of Fire for a ceremony to commune with the ancients. I told him I would bring the peyote and meet him there. I know we aren't allowed to camp in Mouse's Tank, but I'm bringing along my sleeping bag. It will give us something to sit on during the ceremony. Hopefully he'll be able to cleanse our souls for our parts in the murder of Nancy Callahan.

"What a son of a bitch," Rhonda said once she put aside the journal. "Burton had him come out there so he could be murdered. Considering George Spanton is also dead, it looks as if he's trying to kill off all the people involved in Jerry Kaiser's murder. I think it's more important than ever to find Williams, Knilans and Roberts. Hopefully they're all still alive."

~ * ~

By the time Rhonda returned home that night she was completely exhausted. It was rewarding to have the mastermind behind all the murders in custody but at the same time she felt as though she'd opened a Pandora's Box and there was still more she had to do.

"Rough day?" Mark asked as soon as she walked in the door.

"That doesn't even begin to describe it."

Mark smiled at her comment. "I figured as much when I heard there had been an arrest made in the Callahan case. Do you think you got the right guy?"

Rhonda nodded. "We found journals Roger Jenkins kept and found some incriminating information in them. So far, we've been able to pin at least four murders on our suspect and I'm sure there will be a lot more."

"More?"

"We have a feeling this man is responsible for at least twenty more murders across the country. We think the first murder took place in this area and so did the last three, so we have the first bite of the apple on this one, so to say."

"Do you think he was responsible for the murder in Wisconsin you talked to Phil about?"

"I'm fairly certain he is. Once I know for sure, I'm going to have to call Phil and let him know what we've found here. Hopefully, he can get the young man they convicted of this out of prison. If we can overturn his conviction, we can also close a lot of cold cases around the country. I'm pretty sure we have enough evidence, but I'd like to find the other people involved in the first murder and see if they can shed some more light on these cases."

"Well, for tonight let's forget about your work. I have some chicken to put on the grill. While I'm getting it done, why don't you get comfortable and help yourself to the sangria and munchies I have out on the patio."

After changing into jeans and a tee shirt along with sandals, Rhonda went out to join Mark on the patio. She smiled at the pitcher of Sangria sitting on the table next to a plate of cheese and crackers. Just tasting the wine took her back to the night they'd gone to Firefly and enjoyed Sangria with bacon wrapped dates. Even though she'd enjoyed the exotic treat, the cheese and crackers were definitely a Wisconsin treat that reminded her of home.

"I didn't ask, how was your day?" she inquired after taking her first sip of wine.

"It was good. I started working with the basketball team, even though the season won't be starting for a while. It was good to get to meet with the kids. I also helped out with the football team at their practice. They've got a good coach and probably don't need me, but it's good to work with the other coaches. It could help once we get into the season. Now that's enough shop talk."

Rhonda giggled. "We did say we wouldn't talk about work, didn't we?"

"We most certainly did. I was wondering if you would be up for a road trip this weekend. If you can get off, I thought maybe we could take a drive over to Laughlin as well as Bullhead City."

As much as Rhonda would have liked a quiet weekend at home the thought of exploring her new home state with her husband, who was also her best friend, caused a bubble of excitement to begin to grow. "Are we talking a whole weekend away?"

"I can tell you haven't looked at a map of Nevada. It's not that far away that we'd be gone overnight. I figured we could do our exploring on Saturday and spend Sunday relaxing. I know this has been a rough week for you and from what you've said things won't be much better next week."

Rhonda agreed. With Robert Burton in custody, she deserved a weekend of fun with Mark.

Chapter Twenty-One

Rhonda arrived at the office before either Jenny or Karl. It gave her time to read her emails and listen to her voice mails while she enjoyed her first cup of coffee.

The first email she opened with from the department researching the whereabouts of Darrell Williams, Alan Knilans and Joseph Roberts. The word that Darrell died in a plane crash in 2020 came as a crushing blow. She was thrilled to find out Alan lived in Mesquite and Joseph lived in Cactus Springs.

"Aren't you the early bird," Jenny commented when she entered the office. "Anything good in the emails?"

"It's good and bad," Rhonda said before telling Jenny about where they would find Alan and Joseph.

"Hmmm Mesquite," Jenny replied. "I think that's where we should start. Hopefully Alan will have had a connection with Roger over the past eight years. I say as soon as we get the go ahead from Karl we make our way over there this morning. As for Joseph, maybe Karl would be willing to…"

"I'd be willing to what?" Karl asked as he joined them.

Rhonda quickly filled him in on what she'd learned this morning. "We thought you might want to go to Cactus Springs and talk to Joseph Roberts. The trip out to Mesquite and back will take up quite a bit of our day."

Karl agreed and wished them luck in finding Alan.

The trip to Mesquite along I-15 took them past the entrance to Valley of Fire State Park. As they passed the exit leading to the park, Rhonda thought about the murder of Roger Jenkins. In her mind she wondered if it was possible Alan had some part in the murder.

By the time they reached Mesquite, her mind had been working overtime for several miles. "Do you think it's a coincidence Alan lives in Mesquite and Roger has a second shop there?"

"I hadn't given it much thought, but now that you mention it, there could be a connection. We know they are both connected to the murder of Jerry Kaiser. I'll be anxious to meet him."

The address they were given led them to a small house located behind Roger Jenkins' Native American Artifacts shop. The house looked as though it had been abandoned, but the open front door and beat up pick-up truck attested to the fact someone was home.

After they parked, Rhonda walked up to the front door and raised her hand to knock when a man who reminded her of Roger came out onto the porch. His long hair hung in braids down past his shoulders and a leather headband was wrapped around his head just above his ears. He also wore a pair of fringed buckskin pants with a matching shirt. The only things missing were a feather in his hair and war paint.

"Are you Alan Knilans?" Rhonda asked.

"I'm known as Fighting Bear. There are very few people who call me Alan any more. I have embraced my Native American heritage."

"I see. Do you have an affiliation with a certain tribe?"

"My great-great grandmother was a Paiute princess, if you can believe the stories that have been circulating through my family for years. The story goes that she was seduced by a white man and taken away from her people to live in the white world. I can't claim much more than one sixteenth Indian blood, but it's enough for me."

"We're here to talk to you about the murder of Jerry Kaiser eight years ago in Keyhole Canyon."

The color drained from Alan's face. "I-I don't know anything about that."

"You don't?" Jenny asked. "That's not what Roger Jenkins wrote in his journal."

"Wh-what journal?"

"Maybe we should come inside and talk about this," Rhonda suggested. "There's no need for your neighbors to overhear what we have to say."

Alan stepped inside and allowed them to enter the house. Although Jenny went in first, Rhonda motioned for Alan to follow her. She didn't like the idea of him being behind her since she considered him to be a dangerous man.

The inside of the house was surprisingly bright and cheery. If Rhonda didn't know better, she would have thought a woman lived here.

"We'd like to know what you remember about Jerry Kaiser's murder," Rhonda prompted once they sat at the kitchen table.

"I can't say I remember a hell of a lot about it. If it weren't for the nightmares, I would tell you I hadn't even been there. We were so high on drugs, it's a wonder my subconscious even remembers it. Of course, Racing Horse told me all about it. We went there to consider letting Jerry into our inner circle. Soaring Eagle introduced him to the group and told us he wanted to be able to join us in our rituals. I knew him from when he'd go to a pow-wow with us. He wore great regalia, but that day he was dressed in jeans and a plaid shirt."

"You have great details for someone who can't remember the event."

"It's a combination of what Running Horse told me and what I see in my dreams. That was when Soaring Eagle told us Jerry enjoyed the company of men rather than women and he didn't belong in our group. Running Horse told me that was why we killed him. He also told me if I ever opened my mouth about it, he, along with Soaring Eagle would tell the authorities I was the one who did it. I don't believe it for a minute because in my dreams I see Soaring Eagle plunging the lance into Jerry's chest."

Rhonda was surprised at how forthcoming Alan was. He'd confessed to the eight-year-old murder.

"Just what is your connection with Roger Jenkins?" Jenny asked.

"I help Running Horse with the shop here in Mesquite. I've kept it open since his death and the fire at the main shop in Las Vegas. I make all the weapons for the special orders."

"Out of curiosity," Rhonda began, "what was your major in college?"

"I know you think it's strange I'd be doing something like this with my education, but I majored in Native American studies. I'm one of the best artists of weaponry in the country. If I can see a picture of the original, I can duplicate it."

Alan's last statement piqued Rhonda's interest. Up until now she thought Roger was the mastermind of the ancient weapons used in the murders across the country. Now she realized she gave the man far too much credit. "Where do you have your workshop?"

"I have a small one here in the house, but the larger one is in Running

Horses' shop across the street."

"Can you show us your workshops?" Jenny asked.

"You're here to arrest me, aren't you?"

"Yes, Fighting Bear I'm afraid we are," Rhonda replied. "We are arresting you for the murder of Gerald Kaiser. You have the right to remain silent. Anything you say can and will be used against you in a court of law. You are entitled to an attorney. If you cannot afford one, one will be appointed for you. Do you understand these rights?"

"Anyone who watches TV knows the Miranda rights. Before you handcuff me, I'd be pleased to show you the workshops."

The thought of going into the workshop where there would be tools made Rhonda uneasy. With him asking to go there before he was handcuffed would be nothing less than a rookie mistake. Once there, he could easily overpower one or both of them and perhaps even kill them in the process with not only the tools of his trade but also any of the weapons he was working on replicating for various customers.

Jenny glanced at Rhonda. From the look on her face, Rhonda knew her partner wanted to see the workshops but worried about having Alan get into his element where there were tools he could use as weapons. "We can get a warrant to search the shop as well as your house, but if you want to show them to us, you'll have to be handcuffed."

She could see the resignation in Alan's eyes. Without hesitation, he put his hands behind his back. It was evident his drug use in college took its toll on the man's mind. She doubted he had much to do with the Kaiser murder, but he was there, and it made him an accomplice.

Rather than have him take them immediately to the workshops she reached for her cell phone to call for back up. Before she could get her phone out of the holster, she heard sirens getting closer to the small house.

"I called for backup when you were first talking to Alan. I thought we might need it."

Rhonda let out a sigh of relief.

Within what seemed like only moments, two city police officers along with two county deputies joined them. "Do you need assistance, Detective?"

Rhonda turned to see the first of the two deputies standing behind her.

"Yes, we do. We've made an arrest. We need to have you take our prisoner back to Clark County Jail in Las Vegas while we wait for a warrant to search this house as well as the shop across the street."

"We can help you with that," the female officer from the local police commented. "What do you need the warrant to cover?"

Rhonda thought for a moment before commenting. "We need to be able to access all the rooms of this house, the shop across the street and any outlying buildings in regard to an ongoing investigation of four murders in Nevada and several others in states across the country."

The officer nodded and went back out to her squad car. It took only a matter of minutes for her to return with the print out of a warrant for the search.

"You don't need that," Alan declared as the deputies prepared to transport him back to Las Vegas. "I told you if you would take me there without the handcuffs, I'd show you everything you wanted to see."

"You know we can't do that," Jenny replied. "There's no telling what kind of weapons you have in your workshops. Without you being restrained, we would be putting ourselves in danger."

Rhonda didn't miss the change in Alan's expression. The resignation she saw earlier suddenly disappeared replaced by the eyes of a cold-hearted killer. It was entirely possible he'd become so enthralled by Dr. Burton; he had no qualms about committing murder. If not by doing the murder himself, by creating the deadly weapons used to carry out the crimes.

"You'll be sorry for messing with us," Alan declared. "You have no idea what we're capable of doing. There are people all over this country who can…" He stopped mid-sentence, as though suddenly realizing he'd said more than he should have.

As the deputies took him away, Rhonda pulled out her notepad. *Check college campuses in the areas of the petroglyph murders around the country to see if they have a chapter of the Society of the Arrow.*

~ * ~

The search of the two workshops, the house, and the shop yielded more information than they could have hoped to find. Although the shop and its workshop had already been searched, Alan's house was a virtual treasure trove.

His description of a 'small' workshop was highly deceiving. Even though the house looked small from the street, on the back was a large addition giving Alan a workshop twenty feet wide and thirty feet in length.

The room contained three large worktables each with projects in various stages of completion. Each project had a set of meticulously drawn plans along with photos of the weapon to be recreated and a laptop Rhonda was certain contained information about the person ordering the weapons.

"I need everything in this room to be catalogued and seized," she said to the deputies. "This is going to be quite a project, so we're going to have to call in additional deputies to help us with it. I also want all of the computers seized."

To her left she noticed Jenny standing by one of the tables, a look of horror on her face. Glancing at the table next to Jenny, Rhonda knew the reason for her partner's terror. The weapons on the table included a war club and tomahawk like those she'd read were used by the tribes on the East Coast. Had they allowed Alan to come into the workshop unshackled, he could have easily killed both of them with one or two strikes with the ancient weapons.

"We have a safe over here," one of the officers declared. "Do you want us to take it as well?"

Rhonda went over to see the safe the officer was talking about. Instead of the fireproof safe they'd found at Roger's shop in Las Vegas, this one stood at least five ft tall and probably weighed too much to be easily moved.

"Do you know if there's a locksmith in town? There's no way we can move this out of here today, but I would like to know what it contains."

Within an hour a locksmith arrived and opened the safe. The contents turned out to be very interesting. Along with materials to create the ancient weapons were several bundles of cash. Before taking them into custody, Rhonda counted the money. It came as a surprise when she realized the amount of cash in the safe amounted to over six hundred thousand dollars.

"I can't imagine having that much cash in my home," she said half to herself.

"I'm sure it's like the money we found in Roger's safe deposit boxes. They didn't want to have to claim it on their income taxes so it was easier to squirrel it away, so no one knew it existed."

Rhonda pulled another box from the top shelf of the safe. "I think I know where all the money is coming from," she announced. "This box is filled with cocaine and there are several other boxes on the same shelf. I wouldn't be surprised if we found peyote as well as other illegal drugs. These boxes should be sent to the lab so they can be analyzed and identified."

The deputies agreed and secured all the drugs to be sent back to the lab. Rhonda knew with the number of drugs they'd confiscated, a major drug ring had been closed down.

~ * ~

They finally arrived back at the office at three in the afternoon. Karl greeted them with news of his own. He'd managed to track down and arrest Joseph Roberts for the murder of Gerald Kaiser. After searching the ranch, he found not only ancient weapons but also drugs and a cache of money totaling over two hundred thousand dollars.

"I think you've uncovered quite an operation here. When I got to the Roberts' ranch I found one of the most run-down ranches I've ever seen. When we executed the search warrant, I located a greenhouse for growing pot on the back of the property and another area where he was growing peyote cactus. At least we know where Roger got his peyote. As for Joe, he was definitely a throwback with the braids and buckskins."

"Were you able to get any information from him?" Jenny asked.

"Not really. He contends he doesn't remember anything about what happened at Keyhole Canyon other than what Soaring Eagle and Running Horse told him and what he remembers in his dreams."

"Sounds familiar," Rhonda commented. "That's the same thing we heard from Alan when we first confronted him. Let me guess, he said it was the drugs they took that erased his memory of the evening."

"Not word for word, but you're close. Of course, once we arrested him, he asked for a lawyer and that was the end of our interrogation. I also met with your prisoner, and he did the same thing. Roberts got a lawyer from here in town and Knilans called one from Mesquite. I decided to wait until the two of you got back and talk to them and their respective lawyers and see if we can get one of them to roll over on the other. I've talked to the DA, and he says he'll be here as well. As late as it is, I've scheduled everything for Monday morning. Our guests might have a change of mind after they spend the weekend in lockup. I also think the two of you need the weekend for a little R & R."

Rhonda nodded, then thought about the notes she'd taken while at Alan's house. "During the arrest, Alan told us we didn't know who we were dealing with and there were people all over the country who could be a threat to us. I'm beginning to wonder if there are chapters of the Society of the Arrow at any of the campuses close to the murders that took place around the country. If they don't have chapters I wonder if Dr. Burton lectured at any of the colleges in those areas."

"Good idea. It could shed some light on the murders. As for the ones here, we know Gerald Kaiser's murder was considered a sacrifice. Nancy's murder was because Burton didn't think the study of the petroglyphs was something proper for a woman to be doing. As for Roger and George, I believe Burton was becoming paranoid and was worried they'd turn against him. If we hadn't taken him into custody, I'm certain his next victims would have been Joe and Alan. He's escalating. It's best we keep him locked away where he can't hurt anyone else. As for contacting the other states, I'll have the IT department get on it right away. We should have more answers by the time we get here on Monday."

Chapter Twenty-Two

After her weekend of sightseeing and relaxing with Mark, Rhonda returned to work with mixed emotions. The thought of completely closing the case of the three petroglyph murders as well as the murder of George Spanton was exciting. On the other hand, the idea of another confrontation with Dr. Burton or even Alan made her stomach churn uncontrollably.

"How was your weekend?" Jenny asked as soon as Rhonda arrived at the office.

"Mark and I did some sightseeing on Saturday and relaxed on Sunday. What about you?"

"My boyfriend surprised me with a weekend at the Mirage. He said he thought I deserved to be pampered. I have to admit I could easily get used to that lifestyle. He actually won it when he called in to a radio show with a trivia answer. The prize he originally won was dinner for two at our choice of one of the restaurants at the Mirage. Later, his name was put in a draw for the grand prize, and he was the winner."

"Sounds great to me. Since you got here before me did you hear anything about our case?"

"Not yet, but I'm sure we will soon."

Karl joined them. "I'd like you to come to my office so I can bring the two of you up to date on what forensics came up with over the weekend."

Rhonda picked up her notepad and pen before following Karl down the hall to his office. A thick file was on his desk, so she knew there had been several changes in their case over the weekend.

Karl motioned for them to be seated in the chairs in front of his desk. "I got a call on Saturday and came in to check out what we received from the lab. The DNA on the butt of the marijuana cigarette doesn't belong to Robert Burton, but it is a match for Joseph Roberts. That said, I sent a team out to see if the tires on his truck were a match for the tread marks left in the area where you found the butts. I got the results this morning and they are a perfect match. That said, Roberts was out there when Nancy was killed. He's the one I want to talk to first, with his lawyer present, of course. Even though we know, from Roger's journals, that Burton was the murderer, it won't hurt to make Roberts believe we're going to charge him with Nancy's murder."

Rhonda knew her eyes were wide with wonder at what her boss just told her. After reading Roger's journals, she had no doubt Burton killed Nancy because he didn't like having women study the petroglyphs, but she never thought there might be more than one person involved.

"What about Rhonda's idea concerning the Society of the Arrow and the murders around the country?" Jenny asked.

"I have information on that as well. About half of the locations had chapters of the group. The ones that didn't, have records that Dr. Burton was lecturing at their campuses around the time of the murders."

Rhonda smiled as the pieces began to fall into place and close the noose around their prime suspect, Dr. Robert Burton.

Twenty minutes later they were in an interrogation room along with Joseph Roberts, his lawyer and the district attorney.

"You know we have nothing to talk to you about," Joseph's lawyer began.

"We asked you to come here to talk about the new charges being brought against your client. We thought you should know in addition to the charges of attempted murder in the Gerald Kaiser case we're charging your client with the murder of Nancy Callahan at Red Rock Canyon last week."

In much the same way as Alan's had, the color drained from Joseph's face. "I didn't have nothing to do with that murder. It was all Soaring Eagle's doing. Whenever he comes to Las Vegas, he has me take him to Rocky Gap Road so he can hike into Red Rock to worship at the petroglyphs on Sunday mornings. I took him out there and came back a few hours later to pick him up. The last time I took him out there I was really getting pissed because he was so late in getting back that Sunday. When he did come back, he had blood all over his shirt and pants. When I asked him what happened, he told me not to ask questions and got in the truck. I took him back to my place where he immediately burned his shirt and pants. I knew something was up because it was a new outfit he had just bought over at Running Horse's place. I know he paid through the nose for it, but he said it didn't matter because it was something he wanted, along with that new headdress he'd just ordered."

Rhonda exchanged glances with Karl and Jenny.

"Just when did you know about the murders?" the DA pressed.

"You don't have to answer that question," Joseph's lawyer said.

"Just shut up. I didn't know anything about it until after we got home, and Soaring Eagle told me what he'd done. Other than driving him out there, like I'd done dozens of times before, I had nothing to do with it. I'm not going to have that murder pinned on me."

"Do you want to tell us what you know about the Kaiser murder?"

"What kind of a deal will you give me?"

The DA tented his fingers and stared at them as if contemplating his answer. "If you will plead guilty to the crime of possession of drugs with intent to distribute, we will drop the other charges, providing you tell us everything you know about Dr. Robert Burton."

Two hours later, Joseph confirmed everything Roger wrote in the journals concerning the man they'd come to equate with Soaring Eagle the Native American name he'd taken when he started the Society of the Arrow.

"We have everything you told us on tape," the DA advised Joseph. "Once we have it transcribed, we'll ask you to sign it. As part of your plea deal, we will also expect you to testify at the trial of Dr. Robert Soaring Eagle Burton."

Rhonda watched as Joseph's face once again drained of color. She wondered if he would deny everything, he had just told them and further stall their investigation.

"I agree. It will be hard, but I know what Soaring Eagle has been doing was wrong. I got sucked into the idea of Native American history in college then the drugs pulled me further down. Soaring Eagle has been threatening to tell people I killed Jerry Kaiser eight years ago ever since it happened. I think it's a relief to finally be able to put everything behind me. I never remember what happened and I think that's what he was hoping for. I merely believed what he told me and that my imagination took over from there. As for the drugs, it was easier to grow them for Soaring Eagle than to risk facing the death penalty."

~ * ~

After breaking for lunch, Alan Knilans was given the same offer as they'd made to Joseph Roberts. With the threat of the death penalty taken off the table, he like Joseph made a similar statement. The only difference was his knowledge of the reasons behind the murders of Roger Jenkins and George Spanton and the fact both had been carried out by Soaring Eagle, as both of the prisoners referred to Bob Burton. He also said he didn't go to the police because he feared retaliation for his actions.

"I just didn't want to die in the same way as the others. I've lived as a Native American all my life and I know the murders Soaring Eagle carried out were done in a very painful way. I'm just glad this is all over. I can even do the time for the drug charges."

As soon as Alan agreed to sign the statement of everything he said, Rhonda breathed a sigh of relief. She'd been involved in murder cases in the past but nothing of this magnitude.

Once back in her cubicle, she took out her cell phone and called Phil. With the time difference, she knew he'd be home from work and getting ready for a relaxing evening.

"It's over," she said as soon as he answered. "We've proven Ronald Slick Beaver's innocence."

"Are you sure?" Phil inquired.

"Positive. We have written proof in the journals we found in a safe deposit box last week. This morning, two of the other suspects took a plea deal, since they didn't have anything to do with the murders, and they confirmed everything. With these arrests we've solved over twenty cold cases including one right here in Nevada. The man behind this is nothing short of a monster."

"That's right, you were going to get me a picture to take over to Ronald. I never got it."

"There wasn't time. Everything went so quickly once we identified Dr. Robert Soaring Eagle Burton, there just wasn't time. I hope you'll be able to get the news to Ronald and get him released as soon as possible. I do know our department is contacting all the states where the other murders took place."

Epilogue

Rhonda and Mark waited in the baggage claim area of the Las Vegas airport for the passengers from Wisconsin to arrive. She smiled uncontrollably when she saw not only Phil and Judy but also Ronald and his grandmother.

"It's so good to see you as a free man," she declared, as she shook Ronald's hand.

"I have you to thank. When Phil said we could come out for the sentencing portion of the hearing, we were thrilled. If it hadn't been for you, I would have never been a free man again."

"Are you running the museum?"

Ronald smiled broadly. "Grandma and I will open for business after the first of the year. We've been cleaning up several of the exhibits and including a memorial to the young man who was murdered at the site of the rock paintings."

The idea of such a memorial was very touching to Rhonda.

~ * ~

On the morning of the sentencing portion of the hearing, the court room was packed. Not only had people come from Wisconsin but there were representatives from the other states where Dr. Burton committed the murders. Also in the gallery were the families of both Jerry Kaiser and Nancy Callahan.

Since the evidence against him was so overwhelming, Burton pleaded guilty, leaving only the sentencing decision of the judge to be handed down.

Before any sentence was imposed, the victims of the crimes or at least their families were allowed to address the court. The heart wrenching stories coming from the families tugged at Rhonda's heart strings. There were so many of them she didn't know but listening to the Callahans and the Kaisers, to say nothing of Ronald Slick Beaver, brought her to tears.

Once everyone had a chance to speak, the judge asked Burton to stand. "Dr. Burton, you have heard the families tell you of the anguish you have caused them by your actions. In light of those statements, I now sentence you to death."

To everyone's horror, Burton grabbed his chest and collapsed. Although the paramedics were called immediately, they were unable to revive him. God took the sentence of death literally and the man died of a massive heart attack.

~ * ~

"It wasn't the ending I'd hoped for," Rhonda admitted as they drove Phil and Judy back to the airport.

"I know. I wanted the man to suffer, but the result was the same. At least Ronald and the others won't ever have to worry about what the man will do next. I wonder how many other crimes he committed that we didn't know about."

Rhonda agreed. She was glad Phil and Judy had been able to spend a few days with them even though Ronald and his grandmother returned to Wisconsin the morning after the hearing. As much as she missed her friends as well as her life in Wisconsin, Rhonda knew her future lay in Nevada. On their first case together, she and Jenny proved they were one hell of a team and would continue to work well together as detectives for Clark County.

Man in the Lake
The Rhonda Pohs Mysteries Book One

Rhonda Pohs has been hired as a token woman on a small-town police force. Other than traffic stops on the highway, her only other duties are to meet with families after a loved one has been killed in a traffic accident. A call from a distraught wife about her missing husband comes in just before one of a man floating in a local lake. Chief Franks sends Rhonda to check on one of the most cheating husbands in town. While Rhonda is talking to Kitty Reedman, she is informed that the man floating in the lake is Karl Reedman, Kitty's husband. From the get-go, Rhonda is embroiled in solving the mystery of Karl's murder at the risk of her life.

Chapter One

Jack Franks sat at his desk. His name plaque indicated he was the 'Chief of Police' and his uniform denoted his position. Unfortunately, his daily routine seemed about as exciting as watching grass grow on a hot summer afternoon.

He thought of all the episodes of *Law and Order* he'd watched over the years. Now those cops were doing real police work. They certainly weren't filling in for the crossing guard or helping Maude Paul get her cat out of the tree growing next to her porch.

It wasn't like he wanted to have an unsolved murder on his hands, but he did want to do more than act like Barney Fife on the old *Andy Griffith Show*. His officers were good at catching speeders in the speed trap out on the highway, but they did little else to earn their salaries.

Jack heard the phone ring but ignored it. The office employed a secretary and that at least gave her something to do with her time every day.

It's probably another cat stuck in a tree. Certainly nothing to get excited about.

He went back to reading yesterday's weekly paper that just made it to his desk this morning. The news wasn't much different from what they published last week. Clara Johnson had her in-laws over for Sunday dinner so they could see the new baby and the Bradley twins celebrated their sixteenth birthday. Pete Brown's daughter got married and Harley Sacks' dog bit the mailman.

Rather than read anything further, he threw the paper on the desk and was set to go out for a walk when the phone on his desk rang.

"I think you ought to take this one, Chief," the secretary said through the intercom.

Jack sighed deeply and picked up the receiver. "Franks here."

"Jack, this is Al. I just went out to Storrs Lake fishing and there's a man floating in the middle of the lake."

The panic in Al's voice was enough to send chilled shockwaves through Jack's body. "What do you mean there's a body floating in the lake?"

"Just what I said, asshole. I came out to fish and there's a body out in the middle of the lake. I haven't tried to go out and bring him in. He must have drowned. I've seen enough cop shows to know you don't touch things at a crime scene."

Jack rolled his eyes. He and Al had been friends since kindergarten and Al tended to exaggerate. If his friend were a woman, Jack's wife would have called him a 'drama queen'.

"Are you sure some kids didn't steal a mannequin from the mall and dump it into the lake?"

"Mannequin, hell, this ain't no mannequin. It's a man, and he's dead, I tell you. Now get your ass out here and investigate. That's your job, after all. You should do something to earn your pay other than just sitting in the office reading the paper."

Jack shoved the paper aside, ashamed everyone knew about his duties and reading the paper was about all he had to do on a Friday morning.

"Okay, I'll humor you, but if this is one of your practical jokes, so help me Hannah, you'll pay."

He hung up the phone, but it rang again before he had the chance to grab his keys and head out the door.

"This is another one for you to take," the secretary assured him.

"Franks here," he said, just as he always did when he answered the phone.

On the other end of the line, he could hear a woman crying. "This is Kitty Reedman. My husband, Karl, is missing."

Jack thought about Karl Reedman. He was hardly what anyone would call a 'faithful' husband. He recalled how Karl cheated on his first wife, Barbara, with his second wife, Marie. True to form, he cheated on Marie with his third wife, Christine. Just lately, he cheated on Christine with his current wife, Kitty, so why was Kitty so upset about him staying out all night? He was probably scouting out wife number five.

Envy was the word crossing Jack's mind when he thought about Karl's sexual exploits. The man had to have the stamina of a bull in a field full of cows in heat. The thought of a man being able to satisfy more than one woman at a time was mind-boggling. Hell, he had enough trouble with his wife of thirty years, to say nothing of having another on the side and probably out looking for the next sexual conquest.

"What do you mean he's missing, Kitty?"

"Oh, Jack, it's so terrible. Karl went out last night to get a pack of cigarettes and he never came back."

"Are you sure he's not with a friend?"

"Positive. I know what you're thinking. I know all about Susan Barclay. I called her and she hasn't seen him either. We have an open marriage. I know he has the sexual appetite of a much younger man, and one woman is never enough for him. That's why his first three marriages failed. He's not with his girlfriend and we're both worried. We've been calling everyone we could think of all morning, and no one has seen him."

"I'll investigate it, Kitty. I have something else to do first, then I'll be right over to file a missing person's report. I'll see you in a couple of hours."

He hung up the phone and wondered where in the hell he was going to find a missing person's report form. He knew they were somewhere in the office, but since his secretary, Melissa, arrived and reorganized the filing system, he couldn't find a damn thing.

"I need a missing person's report form," he said as he approached

Melissa's desk. "Do you have any idea where I might find one?"

Melissa smiled in a way that said she knew exactly where to look. Damn, he hated the way she smiled when she knew where something was, and he didn't.

She got up from her desk chair and crossed to the filing cabinets. Once there, she pulled open the one with the big black 'M' printed on the little card in the holder on the front.

He watched over her shoulder as she pulled out the file with the words 'Missing Persons' neatly printed on the top cut of the folder.

"Here you go, Chief. Is there any other paperwork you'll need this morning?"

"Thanks. I think this will do it."

He felt a bit sheepish as he left the office and went out to his car. It wouldn't take long for him to get out to the lake. The only thing he would need there was his digital camera in order to take a picture of the mannequin Al insisted was a dead body.

After turning down the road leading past the museum and the industrial park, he headed toward the unpaved portion of the road. When he went to high school, this was lovers' lane. He'd been down there parking with more than one girl when he was the big man on campus, a/k/a the 'captain of the football team'.

Al's beat-up pickup truck sat parked in the makeshift parking lot about fifty yards from the lake. It was here he got caught one night with his girlfriend necking in his '57 Chevy. If Al hadn't come into the parking area driving like a maniac, things might have gone further than kisses and heavy petting. Instead, Al buried his truck up to the axles and Jack ended up helping him dig the damn thing out. To say the moment was lost was an understatement, especially since the girl's father gave him hell for getting her home so late.

"Over here," Al called, as soon as Jack got out of the car.

Jack made his way across the almost knee-high grass, aware of how soggy the ground was from all the rain they'd had this spring.

"I'm coming, keep your pants on. It's so muddy out here, I could sink to my knees and be sucked into the mulch."

He looked past Al and saw the body of a naked man floating face down in the lake. "Holy shit, there's a naked man out there."

"That's what I've been trying to tell you. Do you think we ought to call for the rescue squad to come out here and get him back to shore?"

"How in the hell could someone get out there and drown?" Jack asked. "What did he do, take off his clothes and go out there to commit suicide? He could stand up and the water would be just over his waist. Have you touched anything out here?"

Al looked at him as though he'd lost his mind. "There's nothing to touch except the grass. I did notice some of the grass on the other side of the lake was beat down, but I didn't go over there to look."

Jack shifted his gaze from the tanned body and white ass of the man floating in the lake. The morning sun was doing its magic bringing the bent grass back to standing straight and tall.

Knowing the victim wasn't going anywhere, he left Al and headed around to the other side of the lake. Since the only access to that area was through the gravel pit, he knew he'd have to look there as well. Jack thanked his lucky stars there'd been no rain, as droplets of blood clung to the grass, indicating the path the body was dragged to get to the lake.

After taking several pictures, he turned on his cell and called the county sheriff's office. There was a fine line where this crime was concerned. Technically, the lake was within the city limits, but the gravel pit sat in the jurisdiction of the county. With the body being found in the city limits and the scene of the crime in the county, he knew the investigation would be a joint effort.

An hour later, several deputies, as well as the sheriff joined Jack.

"What made you decide this wasn't a simple drowning, Jack?" Sheriff Cantwell asked.

"It was Al Pardee who first saw the body. When he got out here, he said the grass on this side of the lake was bent. I decided it was best to come over here and investigate since the body wasn't going to get away from me."

The sheriff nodded. "Do you have a boat you can take out there and retrieve the body?"

"I can tell you aren't from town. The entire lake is only waist deep. You can't launch a boat in anything that shallow."

"Just how the hell do you expect to get the body to shore?"

Jack was getting more and more annoyed with the sheriff. The fact he said 'you' rather than 'we' irritated Jack.

"I can check and see if Al has waders in his truck. If he does, I'll go out there and pull the body to shore."

The sheriff looked at him as if he'd lost his mind.

"Do you have any better ideas on how we can reel him in?"

"I hadn't given it much thought. I figured we'd just go out there in a boat and get him. Guess it's a bit more complicated than I thought."

"Look Sheriff, I've been around this lake all my life. Now if it were the lake west of town, your idea of a boat would work. This one is different. If it weren't for all the rain we've had this spring, we'd be looking at a swamp rather than a lake. Calling it a 'lake' has always been a joke. Now if you'll excuse me, I'll go back around the lake and pull in my body."

"Your body? This is *our* jurisdiction."

"He may have been killed in your jurisdiction, but he was dumped in mine. The way I see it, if you scratch my back, I'll scratch yours."

"I'll go with you to make sure you don't muck up the evidence," Sheriff Cantwell proclaimed.

Jack laughed to himself. How in the hell could he muck up the evidence any more than it already was? The poor schmuck had been floating in the lake for God only knew how long. Any evidence would be completely waterlogged by now.

As they headed back around the lake Jack could hear Cantwell swearing about the mud and the muck. It was evident he didn't want to get his highly polished shoes all muddy.

Once back to where Al stood, Jack saw his friend was now grinning like a damned Cheshire cat.

"How do you plan to get him out of there?" Al questioned.

"I'm hoping you have your waders and boots in the truck. It looks like I'm going to go out there and drag him in."

Al laughed, like the idiot he was, and walked to his truck. The damn fool would probably hang around with that shit eating grin on his face until Jack pulled the body in.

By the time Jack pulled on the waders, at least a half dozen officers were standing on the shore, along with the coroner. From the looks on everyone's face, he knew they were grateful he was the one walking out through the murky water. Even though it was only late June, the water was already green. This had been a strange year with almost steady rain combined with an early heat wave.

Even though the waders and boots were a bit too large, it was better than walking out there unprotected. He felt his feet sink into the muddy lake bottom. Slogging through the mud made for slow going,

He finally got to the body and reached out to touch it. His initial reaction was to jerk away from the cold dead skin. With so many people watching his every move, he started back to shore with the dead weight in tow.

Once back at the shoreline, Sheriff Cantwell and two of his deputies helped get the victim out of the water. As soon as they turned the body over, Jack swallowed down the vomit threating to erupt at any moment. Someone had shot the poor bastard in the nuts and cut off his pecker. To add insult to injury, he'd taken a shotgun blast to the face, obliterating his facial features.

"Holy shit, how in the hell are we going to identify this guy?" Cantwell asked.

"That will be my job," the coroner replied. "Between fingerprints and DNA, I might have an answer for you in a week or so."

"A week or so?" Cantwell echoed. "We need answers now."

The radio attached to the sheriff's shoulder crackled indicating a transmission would soon follow.

"We found something over here," the disembodied voice said.

"Don't beat around the bush. What did you find?"

"Well…ah…it's a guy's pecker."

Kitty Reedman's call resounded in Jack's mind. "Ask him if it's pierced," Jack said.

Cantwell looked at him skeptically but repeated the request.

"It certainly is," came the reply. "Not only that, but it's also tattooed with a naked woman."

Jack nearly choked. He'd forgotten the tattoo Karl bragged about getting.

"I'm positive our victim is Karl Reedman. His wife called him in as a missing person right after I got the call about the floater."

Jack checked his watch. "I told her I'd be over there to file a report two hours ago."

"Are you sure?"

Jack wanted to laugh in the sheriff's face, but he remained professional. "Look Cantwell, this is a small town. From the looks of the guy, he's in his fifties, he's going bald, and your boys found his pecker over in the gravel pit, complete with piercing and tattoo. Considering Karl's, the only person in town with the balls to have both procedures done then brag about them, it must be him. Besides, he's a missing person."

"Makes sense," the sheriff agreed.

Jack smiled at the slight victory he'd won over the sheriff in the turf war over this murder. Turning away, he took out his cell phone. Kitty would have to be notified and the best person he could think of to do it was the only female officer on his small police force.

When the city council first suggested hiring a woman, he fought them tooth and nail, but he'd been outnumbered. At least Rhonda was willing to go through grief training. She'd made herself an asset to the department when it came to telling families someone they loved wouldn't be coming home because of a car accident.

About the Author

Wife, mother, grandmother and great grandmother, Sherry is first and foremost an author. She and her husband of sixty years enjoy their retirement and wonder how they ever had time to work. Sherry calls her husband a saint for putting up with an author.

VISIT OUR WEBSITE
FOR THE FULL INVENTORY
OF QUALITY BOOKS:

http://www.roguephoenixpress.com

Rogue Phoenix Press
Representing Excellence in Publishing

**Quality trade paperbacks and downloads
in multiple formats,
in genres ranging from historical to contemporary romance,
mystery and science fiction.
Visit the website then bookmark it.**